THE ORPHIC ARGONAUTICA

AN ENGLISH TRANSLATION

with *selected Roman and medieval writers*
on the voyage of the Argonauts

translated by
JASON COLAVITO

ALBANY, N.Y.
2011

Copyright © 2011 by Jason Colavito

Published by Jason Colavito, Albany, New York

All Rights Reserved. No part of this book may be reproduced or transmitted by any means, electronic or mechanical, including photocopy, recording, or any other information storage and retrieval system, in any form whatsoever (except for copying permitted by U.S. copyright law or by reviewers for the public press), without the express written permission of the author.

This book has been composed in New Athena Unicode

ISBN: 978-1-105-19894-6

www.JasonColavito.com

Contents

Illustrations	v
Preface	vii
Introduction	ix
Note on the Translation	xiii

PART ONE:
THE ORPHIC ARGONAUTICA

The Argonautica   1

1. Invocation to Apollo Followed by Theogony, Addressed to Musaeus, Disciple of Orpheus — 1
2. Jason Entreats Orpheus — 3
3. Catalogue of Argonauts — 6
4. Launching the Argo and the Election of Jason — 10
5. Sacrifice and Oath of Allegiance — 12
6. The Cave of Chiron — 14
7. Leaving Greece — 18
8. The Troad; the Battle of Cyzicus — 19
9. Funeral Games and Purification — 22
10. The Loss of Hylas and Heracles — 24
11. Amycus, Phineus, and the Clashing Rocks — 26
12. Lycus and the Black Sea — 28
13. Arrival in Colchis — 29
14. Achievement of the Fleece — 33
15. Murder of Absyrtus; Northward Journey — 39
16. The Argo Speaks; the Island of Demeter — 44
17. Circe and the Pillars of Heracles — 46
18. Charybdis and the Sirens — 47
19. Alcinous and the Marriage of Jason and Medea — 49
20. Crete and the Return Home — 51

PART TWO:
SELECTED ROMAN AND MEDIEVAL WRITERS
ON THE VOYAGE OF THE ARGONAUTS

The Fabulae of Hyginus 3, 12-25   57

3. Phrixus — 57
12. Pelias — 58
13. Juno — 58
14. Argonauts Assembled — 59

15.	Women of Lemnos	67
16.	Cyzicus	68
17.	Amycus	68
18.	Lycus	68
19.	Phineus	69
20.	Stymphalides	70
21.	Sons of Phrixus	70
22.	Aeëtes	71
23.	Absyrtus	72
24.	Jason and the Daughters of Pelias	73
25.	Medea	73

The Trojan History of Dares Phrygius, Sections 1-3   77

The Narrationes of Lacantius, Book 7: 1-4   81

1.	The Teeth of a Dragon into Men	81
2.	Aeson from Old Age to Youth	81
3.	The Nurses of Liber into Youth	82
4.	A Ram Is Seen in the Appearance of Lamb	82

The First Vatican Mythographer, 23-25, 188   85

23.	On Phrixus and Helle	85
24.	On Pelias and Jason	86
25.	On Jason	87
188.	On Medea, Jason, Aeson, and the Nurses of Father Liber	88

The Second Vatican Mythographer, 135-138   91

134.	On King Athamas	91
135.	On Pelias	92
136.	On Jason	93
137.	On Medea	94
138.	On the Nurses of Liber	94

Appendix A: Translation of Part of the *Argonautics of Orpheus*   99
by William Preston

Appendix B: The Age of the *Argonautica* of Orpheus   109
by E. H. Bunbury

Appendix C: On Valerius Flaccus and the *Orphic Argonautica*   112
by Walter Coventry Summers

Appendix D: On Ireland and the *Orphic Argonautica*   113
by John D'Alton

Index   115

Illustrations

Page xv	Route of the Orphic Argonautica. The reconstruction depicted in this map follows the analysis of Judith Bacon, beginning in Iolcus and moving eastward to Colchis before returning to Greece via the Cronian Sea, the Isle of Circe, and the Mediterranean.
Page 4	Athena helps build the Argo. Roman terracotta relief, c. first century CE, now in the British Museum. (© Marie-Lan Nguyen / Wikimedia Commons. Used under Creative Commons license.)
Page 16	Centauromachy. Attic red-figure kylix, c. 480 BCE, now in the Staatliche Antikensammlungen, Munich. (Public domain image, Bibi Saint-Pol / Wikimedia Commons.)
Page 25	The rape of Hylas. Fourth century CE Roman mosaic from the basilica of Junius Bassus, now in the National Museum of Rome. (Public domain image, Marie-Lan Nguyen / Wikimedia Commons.)
Page 35	Diana and Hecate. This seventeenth century illustration by Wenzel Hollar shows Artemis (the Roman Diana) the goddess of the hunt and her dread counterpart, Hecate, sometimes said to be the same goddess. (Wikimedia Commons.)
Page 38	Jason and Medea. Jason seizes the Golden Fleece from the sleeping serpent as Medea watches. Fragment of a second century CE Roman sarcophagus, now in the National Museum of Rome. (© Marie-Lan Nguyen / Wikimedia Commons. Used under Creative Commons license.)
Page 52	Talos armed with a stone. Obverse of a silver didrachm of Phaistos, Crete, c. 300 BCE. (Public domain image, Marie-Lan Nguyen / Wikimedia Commons.)

Preface

The Renaissance philosopher Marsilio Ficino (1433-1499) wrote that in his youth he had made a translation of the *Orphic Argonautica* from Greek into Latin, but *mihi soli*, "for myself alone." Similarly, the translation offered in the present volume began as a rough English translation I created for my own reference and use in researching Greek mythology. I can make no claim to particular expertise in translation, especially not in the complex and difficult language of the Orphic poem, filled as it is with poor grammar, non-standard word usage, unexplained allusions, many corruptions, and some passages that, frankly, simply defy a translator's ability to make clear sense of them.

Since there is no readily available English translation of the *Orphic Argonautica*, I thought that other interested readers who lack an expert's knowledge of Greek might find my efforts useful; however, I am more than aware that my translation is not without its faults. In no way can this translation be considered scholarly; instead it is intended primarily as a reading copy to give the non-specialist a sense of what is contained in the Orphic poem, long closed to English-speaking audiences. For the purposes of citation or scholarship, the reader should of course refer to the original Greek text, in the modern 1987 edition.[1] In the present volume, I have supplemented the Orphic text with headings to provide easier access to specific passages of the otherwise undivided poem, and I have provided some explanatory notes to help make sense of some of the more obscure passages, and to note where the translation is uncertain.

My translation relies on the Greek text, supplemented by the Latin translation produced by Johann Matthias Gesner in 1764. I also consulted the 1994 Italian translation of Luciano Migotto as well as partial English translations of sections or individual passages by William Preston, Richard Hunter, Radcliffe G. Edmonds III, and others. Where fault remains in my translation, the errors are entirely my own.

---

[1] Francis Vian, *Les Argonautiques orphiques. Texte établi et traduit par F. V.* (Paris: Les Belles Lettres, 1987).

Introduction

The *Orphic Argonautica* (*OA*) tells the familiar story of Jason's quest for the Golden Fleece from the unusual perspective of Orpheus, the Greek mythological figure best known for traveling into the bowels of Hades in search of his dead wife, Eurydice. The first-person account given in the *OA* rehearses the familiar events of the Argonauts' quest—from the building of the great ship Argo to the famous incidents on Lemnos and Cyzicus to the romance of Jason and Medea. In so doing, Orpheus repeatedly boasts of his own prowess and exaggerates his role in events, making himself the most important figure in the poem, an indispensible aid without whom the Fleece could never have been won. The poem also differs from earlier tradition in taking the Argonauts home by a wild and unclear route often interpreted as passing into the Arctic and along Britain and Ireland, which may well appear in the poem under the name of Ierne (see Appendix D).

The *OA* has inspired wildly differing opinions from those who have encountered it. For much of the eighteenth and early nineteenth centuries, the poem was celebrated as among the oldest in existence, behind only the poems of Homer and Hesiod, and thus an important source of information about pre-Classical Greece and even Archaic Greek knowledge of Ireland. By the middle of the nineteenth century, however, scholarly analysis had made obvious that the poem's actual origins were much later, perhaps the fourth or fifth century CE. With the re-dating of the Orphic poem from the Archaic Period to Late Antiquity, the *OA* fell from scholarly favor. One Victorian scholar scoffed that the *OA* was an outright fraud in which "Orpheus himself seriously informs us that he soon expects to reach the coast of Ireland, probably landing at Queenstown on his way to Liverpool!"[1]

Given the hostility Victorian scholars felt for the poem it is perhaps unsurprising that there has been no complete, professional English translation of the *OA* despite modern critical editions appearing in French

---

[1] Alfred Gudeman, "Literary Frauds among the Greeks," *Classical Studies in Honour of Henry Drisler* (New York: Macmillan and Co., 1894), 53-54.

(1987) and Italian (1994), as well as an older translation into Latin (1764). The longest section available in English has long been the three hundred or so final lines of the poem translated by William Preston in 1803 in the third volume of his poorly-received English edition of Apollonius' *Argonautica* (reproduced in Appendix A). Since then, only fragments have been translated into English with three undistinguished exceptions. In 1885, Mrs. Angus W. Hall translated an 1820s German handbook of mythology by schoolmaster Friedrich Nösselt.[2] Nösselt believed the *OA* to be the oldest form of the Argonaut myth, and he drew heavily from it in his description of the Argonauts' voyage. In translating the text, Mrs. Hall accidentally created one of the only reasonably close paraphrases of the *OA* available in English for more than a century. Another was Charles Kingsley's 1856 children's book *Heroes*, which used the *OA* as the foundation for its telling of the Argonaut myth, even borrowing some of the exact language of the poem. An eccentric, self-published 2005 English rendering of the entire poem by Siegfried Petrides[3] received criticism for its difficulties with the English language and the translator's choice to organize verses in a new order to "prove" that (a) the ancient Greeks under Jason had visited South America around 2200 BCE and that (b) all other versions of the Argonauts' story were corruptions of this original, ancient voyage. Unfortunately, Petrides was only one in a long line of investigators to make fanciful claims about the supposedly astonishing revelations contained in the Orphic text, which has been closed to the lay reader without knowledge of ancient Greek except, conveniently, through the work of such spinners of wild theories.

The Question of Age

There is no original manuscript of the *OA* surviving from Antiquity; the poem is known through copies brought from Constantinople to Italy in the fifteenth century—three before 1450, and six more later. Therefore, the poem can be dated only through contextual clues. The author

---

[2] Friedrich August Nösselt, *Mythology Greek and Roman*, trans. Mrs. Angus W. Hall (London: Kearby & Endean, 1885), 309-335.

[3] *Orpheus' Argonautica: A Dissertation on Seafaring of the Late Pleistocene*, 2nd ed. (2006).

of the *OA* claims to be the demigod Orpheus himself, who composed its 1,376 hexameters sometime prior to his death. Thus, the poem asserts that it is a genuine pre-Homeric survival. Of course, nobody bought that. The tenth century CE Byzantine encyclopedia called the *Suda* (s.v. "Orpheus") claims that the poem is the work of Orpheus of Croton, who was said to have lived in the time of the tyrant Pisistratus (sixth century BCE; tyrant of Athens from 546-527 BCE). Later, a school of thought attributed the poem to Onomacritus, a forger of the oracles of Musaeus in the time of Pisistratus (Herodotus *Histories* 7.6.3-5). According to the second century CE Christian writer Tatian, "Orpheus lived at the same time as Hercules; moreover, it is said that all the works attributed to him were composed by Onomacritus the Athenian, who lived during the reign of the Pisistratids, about the fiftieth Olympiad" (*Address to the Greeks* 41).[4] On Tatian's authority, a spurious antiquity was attributed to the Orphic poem. Other accused authors of the Orphic poem have included the fourth- or fifth-century CE poet Nonnus, the author of the eccentric forty-eight book epic poem, *Dionysiaca*, and Cecrops, a Pythagorean philosopher of early date.

A whiff of fraud, or at least something less than the noblest of ideals, clings to the *OA* for many reasons. First, the poem is manifestly fictitious in that it purports, impossibly, to be the work of Orpheus himself. Second, parts of the poem are something less than the original work of the Orphic poet. As André Hurst and M. L. West have shown, a passage in the *OA* describing the mysterious island of Demeter (lines 1199-1202, pp. 47-48 of this edition) borrows (plagiarizes) without significant alteration lines originally used in the lost sections of the *Homeric Hymn to Dionysus* to describe that god's birthplace on Mt. Nysa.[5] Of course, such minor literary borrowings pale in comparison to the debt the Orphic poet owes to his two predecessors, Apollonius of Rhodes and Valerius Flaccus, whose twin *Argonautica* poems were used as the *OA*'s sources, primarily and especially Apollonius.

---

[4] Translated by B. P. Pratten in *Anti-Nicene Christian Library*, vol. III, eds. Alexander Roberts and James Donaldson (Edinburgh: T. and T. Clark, 1867).

[5] Martin West, "The First *Homeric Hymn* to Dionysus," in *The Homeric Hymns: Interpretative Essays*, ed. Andrew Faulkner (Oxford: Oxford University Press, 2011), 42-43.

Literary analysis of the Orphic poem demonstrates clearly that it belongs to the last throes of Antiquity (see Appendix B). While the poem is intentionally archaic in places, mimicking the language and style of Homer, its Greek is clearly archaizing rather than genuinely old, misusing or misapplying older words and phrases to seem like a product of great age. For example, the Orphic poet uses πίσυνος ("trust in") to mean "obedient to" and the Homeric ἀλυσκάζω ("to escape") where the Hellenistic word for loitering is called for.[6] The wording is muddled; the grammar is challenging and confusing, sometimes using incorrect tenses and loose language. In terms of content, the poem's closest relations are epics from the first few centuries CE. Like the roughly contemporary *Dionysiaca* of Nonnus, the *OA* has a greatly reduced speaking role for the gods when compared with its Homeric counterparts, and unlike the Homeric poems, the Orphic poet gave a speaking part to an inanimate object, the wooden beam of Dodona embedded in the Argo, something Apollonius, following Homeric precedent, omitted.

The Argonaut Tradition

The *OA* draws on a rich tradition of Argonaut myths and legends stretching back at least to the time of Homer, and the Orphic poem bears the traces of these earlier works through either the firsthand knowledge of the Orphic poet or through secondhand transmission via the works the poet did consult. It was Homer who first mentioned the voyage of the Argo in the *Odyssey*, around the late eighth century BCE:

> The only coursing ship that ever passed this way was *Argo*, famed of all, when voyaging from Aeëtes: and her the waves would soon have dashed on the great rocks, but Here [Hera] brought her through from love of Jason. (12.69-72, trans. George Herbert Palmer)

The implication of the Argo's fame at so early a date is that the Jason myth was already old. Indeed, as Martin Nilsson first proposed in the 1930s, and later scholars agreed, the Argonaut story probably dates back

---

[6] Hermann Frankel, Review of *Die orphischen Argonautika in ihrem Verhaltnis zu Apollonios Rhodios* by Helmut Venzke, *American Journal of Philology* 65, no. 4 (1944): 394.

in some form to the Mycenaean period (before 1200 BCE). What form that story took, however, is lost to us, though the origins of Jason's name in the Greek word for "healer" suggest that his story must originally have had something to do with healing or perhaps immortality.

The next mention of Jason occurs in Hesiod's *Theogony* (992ff.) of the seventh century CE. In this poem, the characters of Aeëtes and Medea are first mentioned, testifying to their great antiquity. Further references to the Argonauts' adventures exist in the fragments of Hesiod's *Catalogue of Women*. Thereafter we know from fragments preserved in later authors that the Argonaut story remained popular through the Archaic period, including references in such lost epic poems as the *Nostoi* and the *Taking of Oechalia* and in the lost books of such prose writers as Pherecydes, whose work seems to have been followed by the surviving *Library* of pseudo-Apollodorus (1.9.16-28).

However, the story of the Argonauts, unlike that of the Trojan War, existed primarily as an oral tradition, a popular story rather than an elite literary one. The Trojan cycle generated not just the *Iliad* and the *Odyssey* but the six additional epics of the Epic Cycle (seventh and sixth centuries BCE), while the Argonauts by contrast figured more prominently in popular art than in epic. Some have speculated that over time, elite Greek poets came to see the Argonaut story as too suffused with Dark Age ideas of magic and necromancy, associated in later Greece with foreigners and barbarians—inappropriate subjects for the highest levels of Greek poetic imagination. It was only when such barbarities, apparently originally belonging to Jason himself, could be safely transferred to the foreigner Medea that the Argonaut story could become an appropriate subject for elite poetry.[7]

Eventually, the story of the Argonauts was rehearsed, apparently at some length, in the lost *Naupactia* of the sixth century CE, and Eumelus discussed the Argonauts extensively in his lost *Corinthiaca* of roughly the same period. The former poem was apparently the first to continue the story of Jason and Medea past the return to Greece, supplying an early account of the pair's happy reign on the island of Corcyra. The latter poem removed the couple to Corinth instead and apparently originated

---

[7] See, for example, C. J. Mackie, "The Earliest Jason: What's in a Name," *Greece & Rome* 48, no. 1 (2001): 1-17.

the tradition elaborated in Euripides' and Seneca's *Medea* plays that the wife of Jason was a murderess. This line of myth, however, falls beyond the scope of the Orphic poem except for the *OA*'s repeated references to Medea being "unlucky in marriage."

The first complete surviving ancient source for the Argonaut myth is the magnificent Fourth Pythian Ode of Pindar (composed 462 BCE), which told selections from what was clearly a well-developed myth of Jason, placing emphasis on the confrontation between Jason and Pelias that led to the launching of the Argo. In Pindar's version, Jason is depicted as a near-god, almost the equal of Ares, every inch the hero. However, as time wore on, the figure of Jason was increasingly diminished. A wave of rationalizing historians attempted to explain away Jason's story as so many lies and exaggerations. This tendency reached its apex in the work of Dionysus Schytobrachion, whose third century BCE six-book *Argonautica*, now lost but largely followed by the later writer Diodorus Siculus (*Library of History* 4.40-56), removed all references to magic and divinity, instead attributing the Golden Fleece to the flayed-and-gilded skin of a man named Krios (i.e., Mr. Ram) and the fire-breathing bulls of Colchis to a pack of soldiers from the Crimean land of Taurica (which sounds like *tauros*, or bull). Dionysus, however, makes Heracles (a late addition to the myth) the star of the story, demoting Jason to an arrogant and accidental participant in a story meant now to be seen as prologue to the Trojan War. The most important act of the Argonauts in this view was their brief stopover at Troy, where Laomedon, the king, treated them badly and began the mutual recriminations that led to the rape of Helen.

The most important work on the Argonaut theme was undoubtedly Apollonius of Rhodes' *Argonautica*, composed in the later third century BCE. This Hellenistic epic is the fullest surviving Greek account of the Argonauts' adventure, and, if the sheer number of surviving copies and papyrus fragments can be any judge, also the most popular. The poem has spawned dozens of modern critical studies, though such scholarly inquiry is largely beyond our scope. The interested reader, of course, can consult one of many modern translations, including the standard edition translated by R. C. Seaton in 1912 and more recent versions such as that of Richard Hunter. While Apollonius' poem did not become the defi-

Figure 1. Route of the *Orphic Argonautica*. The geography of the poem is difficult, and in places uncertain. The above reconstruction follows the analysis of Judith Bacon, beginning in Iolcus and moving eastward to Colchis before returning to Greece via the Cronian Sea, the Isle of Circe, and the Mediterranean. Other reconstructions identify Lake Maeotis with the Sea of Azov (an arm of the Black Sea) instead of the Caspian, or take the Argonauts further north, circumnavigating Scandinavia.

nitive version of events the way Homer's *Iliad* codified the Trojan War, largely because it came far too late to erase the many poetic and prose renderings that preceded it, in time the poem became the touchstone which all subsequent versions would either follow or from which they must consciously depart. The Orphic poet was no exception, and the echoes of Apollonius are more than apparent in the *OA*, including instances of borrowed language, a close aping of Apollonius' geography on the outward voyage to Colchis, and the order of incidents in the course of the adventure. But the Orphic poet also consciously departs from Apollonius, turning the achievement of the Fleece into a dark, necromantic rite, but most especially in the return voyage, staking out a markedly different route home. The story, from roughly the arrival in Colchis (p. 29 of the present volume), is the Orphic poet's own.

Apollonius' poem was translated into Latin by Varro of Atax in the first century BCE, and Vergil found inspiration for the love of Aeneas and Dido in Apollonius' description of the romance of Jason and Medea. In the reign of Vespasian, a Roman named Valerius Flaccus began, but likely never finished, a version of the *Argonautica* drawn on as many of the preceding versions as was possible for the poet to study, first among which was that of Apollonius of Rhodes. Eight books (of the apparently twelve planned) survive, following the general plan of Apollonius but with details drawn from many other authors. Valerius follows an alternative tradition, however, proposed first by pseudo-Eratosthenes in his *Catasterismi* and repeated by Catullus (poem 61), that the Argo was the first ship. The Orphic poet also departs from Apollonius in the same way, though the *OA* suffers the inconsistency of having the "first" ship land at the port of the sea-faring Phaeacians, chased by the fleets of Aeëtes and his allies. The Orphic poet also appears to follow Valerius over Apollonius in three other details: in making the oracle delivered to Pelias speak directly of Jason by name (Val. Flacc. 1.26-9; *OA* 56-9, pp. 3-4 this volume), in offering a prayer to Poseidon (Val. Flacc. 1.188-203; *OA* 333-352, p. 13 this volume); and the heroes' banquet with Chiron and Achilles (Val. Flacc. 1.252-273; *OA* 376-454, pp. 14-17 this volume). Of course, it is impossible exclude the possibility that both Valerius Flaccus and the Orphic poet derived their stories from an older Orphic poem. (See Appendix C for additional discussion.)

The Orphic Tradition

Given the major sources upon which the Orphic poet undoubtedly drew, one final question about the Argonautic tradition remains: Was there an earlier Orphic version of the *Argonautica* prior to the poem we now have, and if so, did our poet draw upon this earlier source? To answer this, it is necessary to briefly consider the concept of Orphism.

Orphism is the name given to a particular stream of ancient Greek religious thought emerging around the sixth century BCE and attributed to demigod Orpheus. This belief system taught the immortality and transmigration of souls, the importance of an ascetic life, and the threat of punishment in Hades for the sins of this life. The Orphic theology differed from traditional Greek theology in placing its emphasis on figures such as Persephone, Dionysus, and Orpheus himself who descended to the Underworld and returned. By practicing the Orphic rites and being initiated into the mysteries of Dionysus, the believer could expect release from the cycle of rebirth and union with the gods.

Originally, the Orphic beliefs were held close by the Orphics, but over time the principles of Orphism had become known outside of the cult itself. The secret doctrine of the Orphics apparently dealt with the death and resurrection of Dionysus. Diodorus Siculus (4.75.4) reported that "this god was the son of Zeus and Persephone, and born in Crete; and Orpheus in his sacred rites and mysteries, says, he was torn in pieces by the Titans."[8] Zeus killed the Titans in turn with a thunderbolt. According to the myth, after the death of Dionysus, Zeus caused resurrection by implanting the dead god's heart in his own thigh and carrying him to term. The symbolism, then, was of an immortal soul (the heart) held down by the body (the earthborn Titans) until free to join the gods.

Orphism differed from other Greek cults in that it had a vast body of sacred literature from the very first, much of it putatively attributed to Orpheus himself and his disciple Musaeus. Plato confirms the existence of such cult books in *The Republic* (364e-365a), and by the Hellenistic period there was in relatively wide circulation an entire Orphic "bible" known (according to the *Suda,* s.v. "Orpheus") as the *Hieroi Logoi (Sacred Speeches) in Twenty-Four Rhapsodies,* a now-lost collection in twenty-four volumes of reworked older poems, some probably dating back to the fifth century BCE, discussing the creation of the universe and the origin of the gods. The *OA* we possess today reflects this Orphic textual tradition, and its opening passages, discussing the origins of the universe, clearly place it within the context of the *Rhapsodies.* But to what extent did an *Argonautica* already exist in the Orphic canon?

As discussed above, Tatian in the second century CE talks of works attributed to Orpheus, though he does not mention a preexisting *OA* by name. Judith Bacon, in her analysis of the geography of the *OA*, concluded that the confusion of places and events in the *OA* occurred because the late poet was drawing upon an older Orphic version of the Argonauts' adventure, one that featured a shorter route home via the Danube and the Adriatic rather than the North Sea and Ireland. Evidence can be found in the use of vocabulary associated with Orphism, which is much more frequent near the end of the poem than in the sections derived from Apollonius. The implication, Bacon argued, was that an older Orphic poem underlies part (but certainly not all) of the last third

---

[8] Trans. G. Booth (1814), adapted.

of the current *OA*, suggesting a greater antiquity for at least some material contained in the currently-extant text, perhaps dating back to the fifth century BCE.[9] Damien P. Nelis concurred, arguing that passages in Apollonius' *Argonautica* can be read as a reworking of an earlier Orphic poem, probably a theogony (a description of the origins of the gods) containing a description of the epic events of early history, which the current *OA* also relies upon.[10]

Certainly the Orphic theogony contained in the poem's opening has antecedents dating back to the dawn of Orphism. This passage is the most celebrated aspect of the *OA* and has fascinated scholars, especially occultists, for hundreds of years because it is a rare instance of an Orphic theogony directly from the hand of an actual Orphic rather than a non-Orphic commentator. However, the theogony given in the *OA* is not parallel to any one of the six differing Orphic theogonies known from ancient literature and archaeological discoveries;[11] it is instead a literary construct that combines elements of multiple theogonies. Orpheus has long been associated with poetry describing the origins of the cosmos. Apollonius of Rhodes, in the *Argonautica*, has Orpheus sing one vague version of his beginning of things:

> He sang how the earth, the heaven and the sea, once mingled together in one form, after deadly strife were separated each from other; and how the stars and the moon and the paths of the sun ever keep their fixed place in the sky; and how the mountains rose, and how the resounding rivers with their nymphs came into being and all creeping things. And he sang how first of all Ophion and Eurynome, daughter of Ocean, held the sway of snowy Olympus, and how through strength of arm one yielded his prerogative to Cronos and the other to Rhea, and how they fell into the waves of Ocean; but the other two

---

[9] Judith Bacon, "The Geography of the *Orphic Argonautica*," *The Classical Quarterly* 25, nos. 3-4 (1931): 172-183.

[10] Damien P. Nelis, "The Reading of Orpheus: The *Orphic Argonautica* and the Epic Tradition," in *Roman and Greek Imperial Epic*, ed. Michael Paschalis (Rethymnon Classical Studies vol. 2) (Herakleion, Crete: Crete University Press, 2005), 169-192.

[11] Three theogonies (the so-called Rhapsodies, Eudemian theogony, and Hieronyman theogony) are found in the work of the sixth-century CE Neoplatonist Damascius (*De Principiis* 123-124), while three others (the so-called Cyclic, Derevni, and Protogonos theogonies) are modern reconstructions based on allusions, papyrus fragments, and other incomplete sources. The exact details of each are beyond the scope of our inquiry. Aristophanes parodied these theogonies in *The Birds* (698ff.).

meanwhile ruled over the blessed Titan-gods, while Zeus, still a child and with the thoughts of a child, dwelt in the Dictaean cave; and the earthborn Cyclopes had not yet armed him with the bolt, with thunder and lightning; for these things give renown to Zeus. (1.496-511, trans. R. Seaton)

But when the character of Orpheus becomes the speaker in his own poem, his cosmology become far more specific and more Orphic, a full-blown description of the Orphic worldview, replete with references to such figures as Phanes (the Orphic god of procreation) and Brimo (Persephone), cult names associated with Orphic rites and beliefs:

> I disclosed [...] the Great Rites to initiates. Truly, above all I disclosed the stern inevitability of ancient Chaos, and Time, who in his boundless coils, produced Aether, and the twofold, beautiful, and noble Eros, whom the younger men call Phanes, celebrated parent of eternal Night, because he himself first manifested. Then, I sang of the race of powerful Brimo, and the destructive acts of the sons of the Earth, who spilled their gloomy seed from the sky begetting the men of old, whence came forth mortal stock, which resides throughout the boundless world. (11-19; see p. 1-2 of the present volume)

This passage is clearly parallel to both Hesiod's ancient *Theogony*[12] and the Orphic theogony described in Damascius' sixth century CE summary of Orphism in his *First Principles* (123), roughly contemporary with the *OA*:

> They place Chronus (Time) for the one principle of all things, and for the two Ether and Chaos: and they regard the egg as representing Being simply, and this they look upon as the first triad. But to complete the second triad they imagine as the god a conceiving and conceived egg, or a white garment, or a cloud, because Phanes springs forth from these.[13]

In the eighteenth century, the opening of the *OA* was intentionally mistranslated to demonstrate that the *OA* and the Orphic theology were actually a corruption of the Biblical account of the Flood of Noah, with Jason's Argo standing in for Noah's Ark on account of a spurious simi-

---

[12] See note 3 on p. 1 of this volume for Hesiod's *Theogony*.

[13] Translated in I. P. Cory, *Ancient Fragments*, 2nd ed. (London: William Pickering, 1832), 310.

larity in their (English) names.[14] Here is how Jacob Bryant in his *New System* of 1774-1776 mistranslated the passage to relate it to the Biblical narrative:

> After the oath had been tendered to the Mustae [i.e., initiates], we commemorated the sad necessity, by which the earth was reduced to its chaotic state. We then celebrated Cronus, through whom, the world after a term of darkness enjoyed again αιθερα, a pure serene sky: through whom also was produced Eros, that twofold, conspicuous, and beautiful Being.[15]

Bryant here misrepresents Orpheus' description of the formation of the cosmos as instead the degradation of the antediluvian earth (Genesis 6:1-13) followed by a clear sky answering to the rainbow of Genesis 9:13 that God used to make his covenant with Noah. This incorrect version of the *OA*'s theogony was repeated uncritically for most of the nineteenth century by Christian apologists, who sometimes glossed "Eros" explicitly as "rainbow," to "prove" the historicity of Genesis.

If anything, it is the frequent use of the *OA* to support pseudo-historical theories—ranging from Biblical fundamentalism to wild claims that prehistoric Greeks sailed to South America—that makes an English translation essential. So long as the Orphic text remains closed to those not familiar with Greek, those who seek to bend it to fit their theories are able to do so with impunity.

Other Versions of the Argonaut Story

To supplement this translation of the *OA* and to place it in the context of its time, I have included excerpts from additional Roman and medieval texts describing the voyage of the Argonauts in the centuries immediately preceding and following the Orphic poem. I have provided individual introductions to each of these authors, but here a few words about their value in understanding the context of the *OA* are in order.

---

[14] Needless to say, the Ark was not so named in the original Hebrew. The English word is merely a derivative of the Latin word for box, *arca*, of different origin than the Argo, from the Greek for "swift."

[15] Jacob Bryant, *A New System; or, an Analysis of Antient Mythology*, 3rd ed., vol. III (London: 1807), 175.

The three most important Roman sources for the Argonaut story are Valerius Flaccus' *Argonautica*, the various poems of Ovid on Medea and Hypsipyle,[16] and the *Fabulae* of Hyginus. While the former authors are easily available in several editions, the latter is less frequently translated and reprinted. Hyginus' manual of mythology, surviving only in the form of a summary made by a schoolboy, offer several variants not preserved in other authors. Though the *OA* does not evince evidence of reliance on Hyginus, the *Fabulae* serve as a convenient foundation for judging how the "standard" Argonaut myth appeared in the centuries leading up to the composition of the *OA*.

The fifth-century CE *Trojan History* of Dares Phrygius seems at first glance to make direct reference to the *OA* when its narrator (a character from the *Iliad*) asks readers to consult the *Argonautica*, which logically would have to be the story "Orpheus" himself supposedly composed prior to the Trojan War to fit into the book's Bronze Age time frame. But late Antique texts are not always logical, and a better case can be made for this passage referring to Valerius Flaccus' epic. The near-contemporary work of Lactantius Placidus, summarizing Ovid's *Metamorphoses* around the same time the *OA* was composed, is valuable both because it became a de facto manual of mythology by the Renaissance but also because it demonstrates the degree to which the *OA*'s tale was anomalous in the late Antique world, disagreeing as the Orphic poem did with other works of its period.

The two early medieval collections of myth attributed to the so-called Vatican mythographers drew on many of the same sources as the *OA* but evince no knowledge of the Greek-language poem. Instead, they represent a marked degeneration in Western memory of Greco-Roman myth, reduced to a confused pastiche of Latin sources (knowledge of Greek having died out). The First Vatican Mythographer wrote only a few centuries after the Orphic poet; yet so thoroughly had the Roman world passed away that anomalies that would have troubled even the relatively careless Orphic poet stood for half a millennium as nearly uncontested fact until the Renaissance made Greek texts available again.

---

[16] *Metamorphoses* 6.1-349; *Heroides* 6, 12; *Tristia* 3.9.

All this brings us back to where we started, with the rediscovery of the *OA* in the fifteenth century and the efforts of scholars to place it into its historical context and to make sense of a strange, unique text.

Note on the Transliteration of Names

In the following translation, I have employed no single system for rendering Greek names into English. The recent tendency for scholars has been to transliterate Greek names letter for letter, while the traditional norm prior to the twentieth century was to apply English versions, where common, and Latin names otherwise. Neither system is entirely satisfactory. The older system loses much of the flavor of the original Greek by giving the gods their Roman names, such as Jupiter for Zeus, or Minerva for Athena. The modern system is unnecessarily confusing for the non-specialist, giving unfamiliar forms for otherwise well-known names, such as Iason for Jason, or Medeia for Medea.

Where a familiar English name is available, I have generally used it in preference to a transliterated form. Thus, I follow the traditional spelling of Heracles instead of Herakles, Colchis rather than Kolkhis, etc. I have made exceptions where the Latinate form differs significantly from the Greek (obviously, this is a judgment call), as in the Kabeiroi, whose Latin name, the Cabiri, seems to me a bit too Roman for a Greek epic. My non-system, therefore, is to let the text sound Greek while remaining readable for the English-speaking reader. Of course, in my translations of the Roman and medieval writers, the Roman names employed by those authors are retained, and idiosyncratic spellings unique to those authors are preserved.

Part One
THE ORPHIC ARGONAUTICA

Invocation to Apollo Followed by Theogony, Addressed to Musaeus, Disciple of Orpheus

O powerful lord of Pytho,[1] far-thrower, also a seer, whose place is high atop the Parnassus rock, of your power I sing: In turn, may your gift furnish me with glory and send your true voice into my mind so that, by the imposition of the Muse,[2] I may disperse a fine song to the numberless races of men with the help of my well-made cithara. For now to you, O worker of the lyre, singer of pleasing songs, my spirit rouses me to tell of things of which I have never before spoken, when driven by the goad of Bacchus and lord Apollo, I described their terrible shafts, and likewise I disclosed the cure for feeble mortal bodies and the Great Rites to initiates. Truly, above all I disclosed the stern inevitability of ancient Chaos, and Time, who in his boundless coils, produced Aether, and the twofold, beautiful, and noble Eros, whom the younger men call Phanes, celebrated parent of eternal Night, because he himself first manifested.[3]

---

[1] Apollo. Orpheus had met him atop his sacred Mt. Parnassus, the home of the Muses.

[2] Orpheus' mother, Calliope, the Muse of epic poetry.

[3] Cf. Hesiod, *Theogony* 116ff.: "Verily at the first Chaos came to be, but next wide-bosomed Earth, the ever-sure foundations of all the deathless ones who hold the peaks of snowy Olympus, and dim Tartarus in the depth of the wide-pathed Earth, and Eros (Love), fairest among the deathless gods, who unnerves the limbs and overcomes the mind and wise counsels of all gods and all men within them. From Chaos came forth Erebus and black Night; but of Night were born Aether and Day, whom she conceived and bare from union in love with Erebus" (trans. H. G. Evelyn-White).

Then, I sang of the race of powerful Brimo,[4] and the destructive acts of the sons of the Earth, who spilled their gloomy seed from the sky begetting the men of old, whence came forth mortal stock, which resides throughout the boundless world. And I sang of the nursing of Zeus, and of the cult of the Mother and how wandering in the mountains of Cybele she conceived the girl Persephone by the unconquerable son of Cronus, and of the renowned tearing of Casmilus[5] by Heracles, and of the sacred oath of Idaeus,[6] and of the immense oak of the Korybantes,[7] and of the wanderings of Demeter, her great sorrow for Persephone, and her lawgiving. And also I sang of the splendid gift of the Kabeiroi,[8] and the silent oracles of Night about lord Bacchus, and of the sea of Samothrace and of Cyprus, and of the love of Aphrodite for Adonis. And I sang of the rites of Praxidike[9] and the mountain nights of Athela,[10] and of the lamentations of Egypt, and of the holy offerings to Osiris.

And also you learned the multitudinous ways prophesying: from the motion of wild birds and from the positions of entrails; and whatsoever the souls of men prophesy through the ways of interpreting the dreams that pierce the mind in sleep; and the interpretation of these signs and

---

[4] An epithet of goddesses associated with the Underworld. Here, it most likely refers to Persephone, who in Orphic theology was the mother of Dionysus. The "race of Brimo" is Dionysus. The sons of the Earth immediately following would therefore be the Titans, who in the Orphic theology killed Dionysus, prompting Zeus to resurrect him.

[5] The word may also be Meleus; the text is corrupt, and the myth it refers to is unknown.

[6] The founder of the Phrygian mysteries of Cybele, the Great Mother.

[7] Armed dancers who performed in worship of Cybele.

[8] Chthonic deities worshipped in mystery cults on Lemnos and Samothrace.

[9] A goddess of justice, but also an Orphic name for Persephone (Orphic Hymn 29).

[10] The original text reads "Athena," but scholars have corrected it to Athela ("unsuckled"), the mystic cult name Athena shared with Persephone (Athenagoras, *Embassy for the Christians* 20). In context, this seems more appropriate given the mystic, underworld tone of the passage. The preceding adjective, αρεινης, conventionally translated as having to do with a mountain, has been subject to debate due to its particular obscurity.

prophecies; and from the motions of the stars. You[11] learned of atonement, the great happiness for mortals, and of obtaining an accounting of the supplication of the gods, and of offerings to the dead.

And other things were described to you: that which I gained by sight and thought when on the dark path of entering Hades via Taenaron,[12] relying on my cithara, through the love of my wife. Then I described the sacred test of the Egyptians in Memphis that is used to convey prophesy, and I described the sacred city of Apis, which is surrounded by the river Nile.

All this have you learned truthfully from my soul. Now in truth, since a burning passion caused me to abandon this body and fly away into the ample heavens, you will hear from my voice what at first was hidden.

Jason Entreats Orpheus

Once, in Pieria and the highest peaks of Libethra, Jason, first among the heroes and children of gods, came asking me for my aid on his expedition to fetch the fleece with his seafaring ship from inhospitable people, the rich and harmful tribe ruled over by Aeëtes, the son of Helios, who supplies light for men. Pelias[13] feared an oracle that a son of Aeson would take the kingly power from

---

[11] Musaeus of Athens, the disciple of Orpheus, a legendary priest, poet, and seer.

[12] Cape Matapan on the southern tip of the Peloponnesus. Orpheus descended to Hades here in an attempt to rescue his wife, Eurydice.

[13] In most versions of the myth, Pelias usurped the throne of Iolcus from Jason's father, Aeson, variously reckoned Pelias' brother or cousin. The infant Jason had been spirited away to Mt. Pelion, where he was raised by the Centaur Chiron, until his return to Iolcus as a young man, prompting Pelias to conspire to retain power by eliminating Jason. His impious actions earned the wrath of Hera, who was Jason's special protector.

Figure 2. Athena (left) helps build the Argo. Roman terracotta relief, c. first century CE, now in the British Museum. (© Marie-Lan Nguyen/Wikimedia Commons. Used under Creative Commons license.)

his hands, and therefore he devised a trick in his soul so that Jason might die on a fraudulent journey. He ordered that the prince carry back the Golden Fleece to from Colchis to Thessaly. And when Jason heard this unjust call, raising his hands in veneration, he called upon Hera, whom he honored as the most holy among all the gods. In truth, she yielded to this prayer: for she greatly admired and loved the virtuous hero, the celebrated son of Aeson. Summoning Athena Tritogeneia, she ordered the goddess to build the first ship out of wood,[14] the first to pierce the salty deep with its wooden oars, the first to disturb the sea with its passage.

---

[14] The relatively late tradition that the Argo was the first ship began with the Hellenistic *Catasterismi* of (pseudo-) Eratosthenes and was followed by Valerius Flaccus.

When Jason set out to gather the celebrated lords and heroes in Thessaly, he found me occupied playing my cithara skillfully, singing sweet songs, and stroking wild animals and winged serpents. But when he had entered into my unpleasant cave, he returned a gentle voice from his strong chest: "Orpheus, beloved son of Calliope and Oeagrus, ruling the Cicones in cattle-rich Bistonia, I greet thee. I come now to the forest of Haemonius and the river Strymonia and the steep ravines of Rhodopa. I, the son of Aeson, bear the most excellent blood among the chosen Minyans,[15] and I want to be a friend to you: truly, friend, receive me favorably, find my words pleasing to your ears, and give in to my begging. You must go with me so that when returning from the Black Sea and the fortified Phasis[16] in the ship Argo you can show the ways to the Parthenian Sea,[17] a thing wished for by all the heroes, who for that reason are waiting for your tortoise-shell lyre and your divine voice, hoping for your help and that you will share their labor in the sea. They will not undertake to sail to the barbarian peoples without you. And indeed, because you alone among men ventured to the dark fog, down into the bowels of Hades, and found the way back, I ask you to undertake this and make common cause with the Minyans."

I responded to him with these words: "Son of Aeson, is this what you ask me with this exhortation, to help the Minyans go to Colchis, sailing the Black Sea in a wooden ship? Enough work now for me, who has had enough of work; I have attended to all the earth and its cities. When in Egypt and Libya, I came forth as an oracle of men and revealed the secret rites; my mother watched over my furious inspira-

---

[15] The Argonauts traced a common descent from Minyas of Orchomenus.

[16] The river of Colchis, on the Black Sea.

[17] The eastern part of the Mediterranean.

tions and led me thence to another home, where I might come upon old age and the finality of death. But it is not permitted to evade what has been decreed by fate. The commands of fate press down, for these invocations do not spurn the supplications of Zeus' daughters.[18] I will come at once and act as attendant to the younger heroes and demigods. And then I will go to the forsaken cave of my beloved.[19] When the crew sets out I will come to the Minyans on fleet foot through the Pagasetic[20] shore."

Catalogue of Argonauts

There the leaders of the Minyan crew were gathered on a narrow mound of sand beside the river Anaurus. When they had learned that I would be going forth guiding them, they lifted me in an embrace, and every one to a man felt joy in his soul. Afterward, I spoke with these most excellent men. I saw first the strength of the divine Heracles, whom Alcmene bore by Cronian Zeus, when for three days the sun departed and all over was a long night. Tiphys, son of Hagnias, was the helmsman of the long ship. He left the Thespians to work on the waters of Teumessia near the mountain of poplars. He

---

[18] The Fates.

[19] I.e., Orpheus will return to the cave of Taeneron, the last place he saw Eurydice. Orpheus had bargained with Persephone for her return on condition he not look back to ensure she followed him from Hades. When he glanced backward, she was forever lost.

[20] The town of Pagasae, on the Gulf of Pagasae, provided Iolcus, and all Thessaly, with its only harbor. It was the traditional site where the Argonauts' voyage began; however, in the Mycenaean Age, the shoreline had been closer to Iolcus itself.

knew the painstaking art of discerning from the bellowing and flashing of storms when and how to guide the ship.

I became acquainted with Castor, the tamer of horses; and Polydeuces; and Titaresian Mopsus, whom Aregonis the wife of Ampyx gave birth to under a cloak; and Peleus, the illustrious son of Aeacus of Aegina, who ruled over the Dolopes in Phthia. I also saw the noble triple progeny of Hermes: Aethalides, born by the renowned Eupolemeia, daughter of Myrmonides, on rocky Alope; then Erytus and beautiful Echion, who once were born to the lord of Cyllene by the Nymph Laothoe, daughter of Meretus, bearing the golden wand of the Argus-slayer.[21]

Then came Coronus, the most ravenous of the sons of Actor. A bit later came Iphiclus, son of noble Phylacus and Butes son of Aeneus, resembling golden Phoebus. From Euboea came the son of Abas, Canthus, who was killed in Libya. Phalerus, son of Alcon, came from the river Aesepus. He founded the city of Gyrton surrounded by the sea. Next I observed Iphitus, son of Naubolus, who ruled over Phocis and the fortified tower of Tanagra. Laodocus, Talaus, and Areius came, the famous sons of Bias by Pero. Iphidamas,[22] son of Aleus, also came. His mighty father felt sorry for him, leaving behind Tegea.

Erginus came also, leaving behind the fruitful land of Branchus and the ramparts of fortified Miletus, where the wandering river Maeander gushes forth. One of the sons of Neleus, Periclymenus, came forth from far off Pallene and well-watered Lapaxus, leaving behind the city of Aphneus and the mountains of Colona. From Calydonia swift Meleager

---

[21] Hermes, who slew the hundred-eyed monster Argus Panoptes ("the all-seeing").

[22] Usually called Amphidamas in other sources (Pausanias 6.4.6; Apollonius of Rhodes 1.163; Hyginus *Fabula* 14).

approached. His parents were Oeneus and Althaea of the rose-colored arms. Formerly, Iphiclus had joined with his relative Meleager and had taught him to fight. Asterion also came, the illustrious son of Cometes, who lived where the river Peiros flows into the Enipeus and the pair are mixed by the river god Peneus and sent to the sea. Eurydamas came from the wetlands beside the Boebeis and the charming town of Meliboea.

Then came Polyphemus, son of Elatus, whose courage was the most conspicuous among all the Heroes. There also had come Eneus, son of Caeneus, of whom it is said he joined with the Lapiths and was killed by the Centaurs, beaten and crushed by pine-tree trunks. However, he would not bow down or bend under the strain and went down among the dead under the earth while still alive.[23] Moreover, Admetus came from Pherae, this mortal whom Paean was bound to serve under the command of Zeus for having killed the Cyclops that had killed his son Asclepius.

There also came Actor from Opus, and with him Idas and Lynceus, the only man able to see through the air, under the deep sea, and down into the infernal abyss of Hades. Then Telamon followed, born to invincible Aeacus by Aegina, celebrated daughter of Asopus, on the shore of Salamis. Now came the illegitimate son of Abas, Idmon, born to Antianeira by Lord Apollo on the river Amphryssos. Apollo gave him the power of prophecy and divination in order that he could speak the gods' will to men.

There even came Menoetius of Opus, a neighbor of the Minyans, and the surpassingly noble Oileus, and likewise the celebrated Phlias, the

---

[23] Caeneus was originally a woman and changed into a man by Poseidon. Chiron refers to the battle of the Lapiths and Centaurs later in the *Argonautica* (see pp. 15-16).

born to a Nymph who submitted to Bacchus by the river Aesepus, his body free from all fault and possessed of great judgment. Cepheus also voluntarily came to the Heroes from Arcadia. The elderly father of Ancaeus cast him out from cattle-rich Arcadia to join the expedition. At no time did he wear a woolen tunic; instead he wore the shaggy pelt of a bear across his breast.[24]

After him came Nauplius, son of Amymone, who bore him to the Earth-Shaker.[25] He was of conspicuous virtue and his body was like that of the immortals. Then Euphemus was in attendance leaving behind the valleys and the seas near Therapne. Also there came Ancaeus[26] of Pleuron, who was knowledgeable in the movement of the stars and the heavens and the orbits of the planets and could therefore predict the fate of men. Palaemonius also came, the illegitimate son of Lernus. Because his feet were crippled in a brush fire, everyone called him the son of Hephaestus.[27] And from the Pistad by the river Alpheus came Augeas, son of Helios. In truth, there even came the twin progeny free from blemish, Amphion and Asterius, leaving behind Pellene, their home and fatherland.

I became acquainted with the twin sons of Boreas by Oreithyia, the daughter of Erectheus, whom Boreas seduced by the stream of Hissus and flew up with into the air, causing her to give birth to sons called Zetes and Calaïs, with bodies like the immortals. In truth, Pelias' son Acastus came from Pherae, for he was rejoicing to go to the inhospitable Caucasus with the heroes in the ship Argo. With him came the friend of

---

[24] Ancaeus, son of Lycurgus, wore a bearskin, a symbol associated with Arcadia, and carried only an axe to fight the Calydonian boar. During this hunt, he died.

[25] Poseidon, who in addition to presiding over the sea was also the god of earthquakes.

[26] A second and separate Ancaeus, often confused with Ancaeus of Arcadia.

[27] The craftsman god was lame, a trait associated with blacksmiths in Antiquity.

the divine Heracles, the beautiful Hylas, who had not yet had any down redden the milky white of his tender cheeks and chin; this boy still gave great pleasure to Heracles.

Launching the Argo and the Election of Jason

And indeed this band of men had been called together to the ship, and each addressed those coming, and spoke to them, and made available to one another the hospitality of the banquet table. But after the group had sated its soul with food and drink and had made camp, each man burned with desire to undertake the great work. When they had all gotten up from the deep sandy shore, they went to the place above the sea where the ship had been assembled and they were struck dumb by the sight; but soon Argus[28] revealed an inspired plan to move the ship with wooden rollers, and he had bound the stern with rope. He ordered everyone to approach. They obeyed and pulled off their armor. They bound the ropes around their chests like fetters, and each man pressed quickly into the rapid waves in order to drag the talkative[29] Argo. And her weight caused her to get stuck in the sand, entwined in dried seaweed, not yielding to the combined strength of the Heroes' hands.

Jason's soul froze, and he nodded at me to look at this and rouse the weary men with my robust and lively songs. And I, holding out my lyre

---

[28] The builder of the Argo, not to be confused with the monster slain by Hermes.

[29] The Argo had built into it a plank of oak (or, in the *OA*, beech) from Zeus' sacred grove at Dodona, and this plank was said to speak the will of Zeus.

in my hands, called up the delectable glory of the songs of my mother, and brought forward a sweet voice from my breast: "The heroic blood is manifest in the Minyans. Come now! Press forward with those ropes tied around your chests. Make an attack together. Stretch out the rope by taking steps forward, and draw the ship forward successfully! And you, Argo, built of pitch-black oak, hear my voice, and indeed you heard me before, when I stroked the trees on the well-wooded peak and you descended for me from the mountain to the sea. Follow now the way to Parthenian Sea. Hurry to travel to Phasis and yield to my cithara and my divine voice."

Then was heard the bellowing of the sacred beech beam of Tomarian Zeus, which Argus had placed before the keel of the ship by order of Pallas, and the Argo slipped so quickly to the sea that she scattered the close-set timbers placed beneath her keel, and only one stretched rope was needed. On both sides, clouds of sand rose up in waves, and Jason rejoiced in his heart. Argus leapt into the ship, and Tiphys followed nearby. Then they assigned fitting and appropriate places. They prepared the mast, and sails, and they barred the steering oars, suspended from the stern and bound with a leather strap. Then, with the oars stretched out on both sides, and the Minyans hastening to advance, Jason addressed the heroes:

"Hear me: It does not please me to give orders to you, O mighty lords. In truth, whosoever stirs your heart and soul, set him up as your leader, who shall be careful for everything and take it upon himself to order us to sail across the sea or to put ashore, or to deal with Colchis or with other men. And indeed, determine with me on whom you shall fix this honor. There are many among you who boast of being from the race of the offspring of the immortals. You seek the shared glory of this labor. I am not considered better or more glorious than Heracles, and him you know well."

All recommended, roaring with a great number of voices, that the leader of the Minyans should be Alcides,[30] who was more excellent than any of the crew. But they did not persuade the wise Hero, who now understood by the instigation of Hera that the son of Aeson was to be preferred as the manager of this good and glorious undertaking. And so Heracles announced that the leader of the fifty oarsmen should be Jason on land and sea. And then all gave great praise to what Heracles ordered, and they set up Jason as leader.

Sacrifice and Oath of Allegiance

When the Sun had severed the sky with his swift horses and the dark night stretched out, indecision stirred the breast of Aeson's son about whether he should impose an oath of loyalty upon the Heroes to seal their faith in him. And I say to you, beloved Musaeus, son of Antiophemus, he ordered me to prepare quickly for an appropriate sacrifice. And so I built an altar of excellent oak on the shore, and putting on a robe, I offered service to the gods on behalf of the men. And then I slit the throat of an enormous bull, bending back the head to the gods, cutting up the fresh meat and pouring the blood around the fire. After I laid the heart on broken cakes, I made a libation of oil and sheep's milk.

---

[30] Heracles was called Alcides either because his birth name was Alcaeus or because it was the name of his (adoptive) grandfather, depending on the account.

I then ordered the Heroes to spread 'round the victim, thrusting their spears and their swords furnished with handles into the victim, and into the hide and the viscera shining in my hands. And I set up in the middle a vessel containing kykeon, the sacred drink of water and barley, which I carefully mixed, the first nourishing offering to Demeter.[31] Then came the blood of the bull, and salty sea-water. I ordered the crew wreathed with crowns of olive leaves. Then filling up a golden vessel with kykeon by my hands, I divided it by rank so that every man could have a sip of the powerful drink. I asked Jason to order a dry pine torch to be placed beneath, and with swift motion the divine flame ascended. And this I called out while lifting my hands to the seashore and the sea rich in waves:

"O powerful Oceanus, and the sea churning with waves, the abyss holding the blessed, and all those who inhabit the rough sandy shores and the rock-strewn sea, and the outer wave of Tethys! I call first upon Nereus, with his fifty beloved girls; Glaucus, full of fish; the vast Amphitrite; Proteus and Phorcyn; the broad power of Triton, and the swift Winds, with the breeze bearing winged sandals of gold. I call upon the Stars shining afar, and the darkness of murky Night, and Auge,[32] the forerunner of the Sun's swift horses. May the gods of the sea guide the Heroes over the seas, rivers, waves, and shores. And I beseech the son of Cronus, Poseidon himself, the Earth-Shaker, clothed in blue: may a jumping wave come to aid in our oath, so that the companions of Jason may always remain committed helpers in this task and so that we all to a man may return home! In truth, whoever fails to honor this pact and

---

[31] The kykeon was both the preferred drink of peasants and the sacred drink of Demeter's Eleusinian Mysteries. The goddess refuses red wine but consumes kykeon with mint in the *Homeric Hymn to Demeter* (206-211).

[32] One of the Horae, the goddesses of natural order, presiding over day's first light.

transgresses against it, may Diké[33] bear witness and the Furies destroy him."

And, trembling, they agreed to the oath with one soul, and they gave the signal of their assent with their hands.

The Cave of Chiron

And when they had sworn to the oath, they went down into the ship and took their places and took up their oars in their hands. Thereupon Tiphys ordered a long rope to carry the ship from the harbor to the shore. Then Hera, the wife of Zeus, sent a favorable blowing wind and spurred the Argo on its course. The princes therefore, by their hands and souls, moved the ship with their rowing: The immense sea was cleaved, and foam rose up from the keel. And when the first light appeared newborn from the river Ocean, dawn followed, bringing a pleasant light to mortals and immortals alike. Then the well-wooded, windy mountain of Pelion appeared by the shore. Tiphys adjusted the rudder and ordered the ship to follow the shore for a little while. And thus quickly we put ashore and a wooden ladder was lowered down to the harbor. The Minyan Heroes climbed down the ladder and rested from their labors.

Peleus addressed them: "Do you see, friends, that dark spot on the summit of the mountain? In that cave lives Chiron, the most just of the Centaurs who lived in the cave of Pholus and the high summits of the Pindus range. He gave judgment and treated the sick, and knocked the

---

[33] The goddess of justice.

cithara from the hands of Phoebus with his sweet playing of the tortoise shell phorminx[34] of Hermes. He brought justice to all his neighbors. Therefore, right after giving birth to our child,[35] Thetis of the silver feet bore our boy up leafy Pelion in her arms and handed him to Chiron[36] to rear and educate wisely and well. I wish to see him. Come, friends, let us approach the cave and see my boy."

He pointed the way, and we followed him into a dark hall. There lay recumbent the great Centaur, resting against a rock, his hooves and swift horse feet extended. Standing near, the son of Peleus and Thetis played the lyre with his hands, which lifted the spirits of Chiron. When he first caught sight of the famous lords, he stood up to greet them and kissed each and every man. He made food available and furnished amphorae of wine. He spread out a covering of torn leaves and commanded his guests to take a place. He swiftly placed ample deer and boar meat on rough plates; afterward he distributed sweet wine to drink.

When everyone was sated with food and drink, all simultaneously clapped their hands so that Chiron and I would have a song and cithara-playing contest. I did not want to yield to humor, for I was unwilling and ashamed to risk showing up a man born before me. But Chiron himself signaled his wish to vie with me in song. Before he sang, the Centaur took from Achilles the beautiful lyre which he was playing, and Chiron first sang of the battle of the violent-hearted Centaurs whom the Lapiths killed due to their recklessness, how obstinately they fought

---

[34] A stringed instrument similar to a lyre or a cithara.

[35] Achilles.

[36] The Centaur Chiron has also been Jason's tutor during his exile from Iolcus and, by some accounts, had given Jason his name (Pindar, *Pythian* 4.120 with scholia). Chiron was famous for his medical knowledge, represented in Jason's name (= "healer").

Figure 3. Centauromachy. Attic red-figure kylix, c. 480 BCE, now in the Staatliche Antikensammlungen, Munich. (Public domain image, Bibi Saint-Pol/Wikimedia Commons.)

against Heracles on Pholoe when wine roused their spirits.[37]

Then I picked up my tortoise-shell instrument and sent forth a honeyed song from my mouth: First I sung of the obscurity of ancient Chaos, and how the elements were ordered, and the Heavens reduced to bound. I sang then of the creation of the wide-bosomed earth, and the depth of the sea, and Eros, the most ancient, self-perfecting, and of manifold design. I sang of how he generated all things and parted them

---

[37] The wild Centaurs became drunk at the wedding of the Lapith king Peirithous and tried to carry off the Lapith women. Theseus aided the Lapiths in defeating the Centaurs in a battle known as the Centauromachy. In another incident, the Centaurs attacked Heracles when he was visiting Pholus, a civilized Centaur who lived on Mt. Pholoe in the Peloponnesus, resulting in Pholus' accidental death.

from one another. And I have sung of Cronus so miserably undone, and how the kingdom of the blessed Immortals descended upon thunder-loving Zeus. I then sang of the younger generation of the blessed ones, and of the destructive acts of Brimo, Bacchus, and the Giants. I sang too of the origins of the many scattered races of men.[38]

The sound of my tortoise shell instrument and my sweet voice traveled through the narrow cave and were heard across the peaks and vales of well-wooded Pelion, and my voice entered even the highest oaks. In the deepest roots of Chiron's hall, the very rocks resounded. The wild animals sat outside Chiron's cave listening, and the birds surrounded the Centaur's lair as if their wings had grown tired and they had forgotten their nests. Seeing this, the Cenatur was struck dumb and repeatedly struck hand upon hand and his hooves upon the ground.

Tiphys enjoined the Minyans to go forth from the cave and enter the ship; thus I brought my song to an end. They rose quickly and put on their arms. Meanwhile, Peleus hugged his boy, kissed him on the head and both eyes, tearfully laughing. His mind was soothed by Achilles. Moreover, the Centaur gave me a leopard skin from his hand, to bear away as a gift. As we rushed from the cave, the old Phillyrides[39] beseeched us with upraised hands and called upon all the gods for the return of the Minyans and great glory for the younger princes about to become men.

* * *

---

[38] This passage is a rough paraphrase of the opening of the *Orphic Argonautica*.
[39] Chiron, the son of Phillyra.

Leaving Greece

After everyone had gone down to the shore and into the ship, they took their seats, stretched out the oars with their hands, and struck out into the waves, departing from Pelion. Above the great surface of the sea, the churning foam made the water white. The headland of Pissaeum was hidden, and the bank of Sepia. Sciathus appeared. The tomb of Dolops[40] came into sight, and the seaside Homole, and the rushing river Amyrus, which sends its waters thundering across the land and into the sea. The Minyans saw far off Olympus on account of its inaccessibly high rocks, and they passed well-wooded Athos and spacious Pallene and sacred Samothrace. The Heroes eagerly approached upon my advice this place, Samothrace of the sacred rites of the gods that may not be defiled by men, for great is the utility of these rites to sailing men, and indeed to all men.[41]

We brought our swift ship up along the haughty Sintian coast of holy Lemnos. There evil acts had been done by the women. In their wickedness, they had killed their husbands.[42] Renowned Hypsipyle, the most beautiful of the women, now ruled over them according to their wishes. But, in truth, what is the reason for making a long tale of this,

---

[40] A son of Hermes who was most famous for his funeral monument in the region of Peiresiae and Magnesa.

[41] Samothrace was home to a sanctuary of the Kabeiroi and offered initiation into a mystery cult. One aspect of the Mysteries of Samothrace offered protection at sea.

[42] This mythological event was commemorated at Lemnos in an annual ritual connected to the Kabeiroi and, later, to the Argonauts whereby the island's men leave and later return.

Musaeus, how Cypris[43] nurse of love, excited the desire of the Lemnian women to have sex with the Minyans, so that by magical enticement Jason possessed Hypsipyle[44] and the other Minyans made love with the other women? They would have forgotten about the expedition had I not called them back to the dark ship with my restraining words and soothing song, making them long for their oars and demand earnestly for resumption of their task.

The Troad; the Battle of Cyzicus

Then early in the morning we entered the Hellespont with a favorable wind sent by the powerful Zephyr. We passed beside narrow Abydos, Dardanian Ilion,[45] and Pitye on the right, and Abarnis and Percote, the fruitful land which Aesepus washes with silver streams. And jumping, the talkative Argo hastened at once to where we put her ashore. There, the ship's helmsman Tiphys, the famous son of Aeson, and all the other Minyans raised a heavy stone to gray-eyed Athena (where the nymphs made beautiful waters gush forth from the Artacian fountain) because sailing through the wide Hellespont, the fair weather that had occurred receded and forced them to cast anchor on land as the waves beat down with wintery breath.

---

[43] Aphrodite. The goddess was associate with Cyprus.

[44] Jason had twins by Hypsipyle, including Euneus, who became king of Lemnos after his mother killed herself because Jason broke his oath to return to her. The other son was named Nebrophonus of whom little more can be said.

[45] The city of Troy, the site of the Trojan War a generation after the Argonauts.

There, preparing an eating place and dinner on the high shore, we gave a banquet for all. Cyzicus, the son of Aeneus, who ruled over all the Doliones, came up and took a place among the Heroes. He had been born to a most noble woman, Aenete, daughter of Eusorus. He honored the Minyans with hospitality, slaughtering colored sheep, curved-footed cows, and ferocious pigs. In addition, he gave red wine and sent copious grain for the trip, bringing also cloaks, woolen cloth, and well-sewn tunics. He was surrounded by the assembled guests, who were of similar age, and he feasted and entertained them through the whole day.

But when the Titan Ocean plunged into disorder and the Moon wrapped the stars in a blanket of darkness,[46] there came men of Ares who lived on mountains in the far north, stupid, like wild savages, strong like the Titans and the Giants. Indeed six hands emerged from their shoulders. Observing the invincible lords, they charged in battle wearing the armor of Ares. The strangers fought partly with pine torches and partly with fir spears, and they made an attack on the Minyans through the dark fog. The strong son of Zeus[47] killed the invaders, sending forth arrows; and likewise he killed Cyzicus, the son of Aeneus, not intentionally but through ignorant confusion. Truly, he was fated to be killed by Heracles.

At once the Minyans within the ship met to prepare for departure, and each man took up his rowing position. Tiphys, shouting from the stern, ordered the ladder dragged up into the ship in order to set sail from the coast. In truth, they were not able to loosen the rope, but they were held back by churning waves and an inexplicable knot that had bound them fast. Tiphys, a strong man, was struck dumb and, losing his

---

[46] I.e., a storm churned the sea and darkened the sky with clouds and fog.
[47] Heracles.

speech, dropped the Argo's rudders from his hands, and indeed he hoped the waves would pass away. Certainly Rhea[48] was furious with the Minyans for hewing down her people.

In the middle of the night, when the far off shining stars fell beneath the river Ocean, a deep sleep attacked the eyes of the helmsman. The dread goddess Athena stood near him in sleep, and gave an order with these words of divine rebuke: "Sleeping son of Hagnias, are your eyelids wrapped in sleep? When you arise, Tiphys, you must order the Heroes to return to the tranquil shore, emerge from the ship, and go to the place where the killing occurred and pay homage to the dead. Rhea, the all-mother, orders you to give honors and offerings to those below the earth, and to pour out the tears of your eyes, honoring the divine law and the hospitality of the table. Heracles killed a guest imprudently in the nighttime mists, thus provoking the rage of Rhea. But when you will have justly honored the dead, then at once climb Dyndimon, the seat of Rhea. There you shall find purification from the daughter of Ge. Then finally, you can sail away from the shore." Thus having spoken, the goddess changed into the form of an arrow and shot into the sky.

Tiphys' stupor dissipated at once, and quickly dismounting from the stern, he roused the men with a shout, shaking the sleeping and resting men on this side and that, and he pointed out to them the course they must take. Rising quickly, they jumped down to the shore.

*   *   *

---

[48] The Titan Rhea was the mother of Zeus and the daughter of the earth, Ge. She was often identified with the goddess Cybele and was titled the "mother of the gods."

Funeral Games and Purification

Meanwhile, Eos of the dawn appeared as a thong of gold born from the darkness, and the dawn sky returned. Then the noble Minyans recognized the corpse of Cyzicus, polluted with dust and blood. There lay all around him the bodies of their enemies, the wild and monstrous beasts, but also among them those of some of their allies. Placing King Cyzicus under a wooden plank, they heaped up a mound atop him, and they built a monument. Then they quickly brought logs and burned offerings of black bulls for the dead. I placated the dead king's soul, pouring out rich liquid as a means of appeasing him, water and honeyed milk, just as one should sprinkle a libation on a corpse. And I sang a hymn of honor.

The son of Aeson himself proposed funeral games, and as prizes for the winner of the funeral games the gifts which Hypsipyle had given them on Lemnos. To Ancaeus he gave the prize for wrestling, a very large, golden two-fold drinking vessel. To Peleus, the victor in the foot race, he gave a purple cloak, a product of Athena's many arts. He bestowed upon Heracles, the winner of the gymnastic contest, a silver krater everywhere encrusted with figures. To Castor, the winner of the equestrian contest, he gave a golden decorative horse collar. To the victorious boxer Polydeuces, he gave a woolen cloth embroidered with flowers. Jason himself seized the pliant bow and arrows. He threw a spear, which flew a long way. Therefore the crowd of Minyans gave the son of Aeson a crown woven of blooming olive branches. Finally, Jason gave me a prize for my song to the gods, holding out the high boots worn by poets, these bearing golden wings. Thus ended the games.

Meanwhile, a rumor flew within the king's house that Cyzicus was dead: His unfortunate wife, tearing her breast, cried sharply, and tying a rope around her neck killed herself with the noose. But the earth took in the tears, and there emerged from that spot a fountain like unto a basin from the middle of which forever gushed forth water like unto silver. The people of the area called it Cleite.[49]

Then Argonauts on account of this, which they had heard during their sleep, proceeded to the top of the mountain of Dyndimon in order to avoid the wrath of the most ancient Rhea and placate the goddess by abundant libations of wine. I followed, holding my tortoise-shell instrument in my hands. And Argus came, leaving behind the famous ship. He cut down with iron the trunk of a fir tree surrounded by dry grape vines, and he fashioned this by his art into the image of the goddess in order that it should remain for future men. He built a house of rocks for the goddess. Here, the work spurring on the Minyans, most of all the son of Aeson, they joined together to build an altar of stones on which were added libations and a bull sacrifice. The princes obtained omens from the sacrifice that the libations pleased Rhea. But they ordered me to sing to the goddess and honor her so that she would grant our prayers to depart.

When we had beseeched the goddess with prayers and incense, we descended back down to the Argo. Tiphys had called to the Heroes from the stern, and they took their seats. Settling in to their seats, they began rowing. And now the rope loosened from the land, and the shore disentangled, and suddenly Rhea sent a favorable wind from high atop

---

[49] After the name of Cyzicus' late wife, Cleite.

Dindymon, dressed with splendid towers. We made sacrifices in honor of our return to the ship, having ordered the construction in the temple on Dindymon of an altar of the goddess, to be called among future generations Rhea Pismatia,[50] the goddess of the cables.

The Loss of Hylas and Heracles

When the wind had filled the sails of the ship, it ran, cleaving the salty waves of the sea; and it skirted near the boundary of the Mysians' land. Quickly in its course, it crossed the mouth of Rhyndacos, entered in the beautiful port, and arrived at a sandy shore. Then hurling the rope, the Argonauts fastened together the sails and bound the leather straps. They threw down the ladder to the land, and climbed down, greatly desiring food and drink. Around a hill, there appeared Arganthos and vast rocky peaks.

Heracles hastened to a well-wooded hill, bearing three-pronged arrows so that he might supply food for the crew, such as boar, horned cow, or goat. But Hylas followed him from the ship in secret and wandered off, roaming the woods. He came across a marshy cave belonging to Nymphs. They caught sight of the young man as he went by, and thinking he looked like a god, intercepted him so that he could be immortal with them and be free from old age for all time.

But when the sun drove his swift horses to the middle of the day, suddenly a favorable wind blew from the mountain and cut into the white sails. Tiphys gave the sign to return to the ship and loosen it from

---

[50] Apparently derived from πεῖσμα, or "ship's cable."

Figure 4. The rape of Hylas. Fourth century CE Roman mosaic from the basilica of Junius Bassus, now in the National Museum of Rome. (Public domain image, Marie-Lan Nguyen/Wikimedia Commons.)

the shore. The Argonauts obeyed the exhortation of the helmsman. Polyphemus, son of Elatus, quickly ascended to the top of the mountain, calling Heracles to hasten back to the ship. But he did not run to meet them, for Heracles had lost all strength for continuing on the journey to the beautiful Phasis.

* * *

Amycus, Phineus, and the Clashing Rocks

Near morning, we came to a deadly land where Amycus reigned over the Bebryces. He laid down a law by Zeus Panomphaeus,[51] the source of all oracles, that none should be provided with hospitality until he had challenged him in battle. And so, when the Argonauts came to his house, he sent for someone to put to the test in boxing. The powerful Polydeuces therefore killed him, beating his head (like a thunderbolt) with his boxing glove. The Minyans completely destroyed the crowd of Berbyces with bronze arms.

Weary of rowing, we put ashore at the wide beach of the large city of Bithynios, hurrying through the mouth of the river; and in the snowy woods, we marked off a nighttime camp and prepared dinner. There the unfortunate Phineus, due to the rage of his wife, had blinded his two sons, and enchanted by womanly words, he abandoned them on nearby rocks to become prey to wild beasts.[52] The two sons of Boreas found them unharmed, and, enraged, they in turn brought punishment to Phineus, taking away the splendor of light from his eyes. Afterwards, violent Boreas[53] threw up a storm full of whirlpools in the dense forest of

---

[51] Zeus as the god of "all signs and omens," whose sanctuary was between capes Rhoeteum and Sigeum (cf. Homer, *Iliad* 8.250).

[52] Several versions of the story of Phineus's blindness were told. In other versions, he is blinded for revealing the gods' will (Apollodorus 1.9.21) or by Helios, carrying out a curse Aeëtes put upon him for rescuing the sons of Phrixus Aeëtes tried to kill (scholia on Apollonius of Rhodes *ad* 2.207).

[53] Boreas was Phineus' father-in-law and thus the grandfather of the boys Phineus tried to kill, explaining his particular desire for revenge. Zetes and Calaïs were the boys' cousins.

Bistonia, where through the storm's destructive strength, death overtook Phineus.

Then leaving behind the house of Phineus, son of Agenor, we crossed the surface of the great sea and came to the Cyanaean rocks,[54] about which my mother, the farseeing Calliope, had told me. Truly there was no place of refuge, but impelled by a frothing wind storm, their clashing would destroy us as we went through. The crash sent waves through the sea and the spacious sky and stirred up the waters in such a way that the boiling sea made much noise with its immense waves. I predicted to Tiphys, son of Hagnias, that he should look back at the stern and beware. His soul was struck dumb by what he heard, but in his breast he hid from the Heroes that which would happen.

And gray-eyed Athena, by the instigation of Hera, sent a heron so that it could be brought up to the highest yardarm. It reluctantly flew toward the danger: It turned around the innermost rocks with is upraised wings, and the shaking rocks rushed into one another and clipped the end of the bird's tail; moreover, in vain did the rocks strike each other in turn. Tiphys, when he saw the heron plunge headlong into danger, urged on the heroes with a silent signal. Realizing they were being sent forth and urged on, they cleaved the waves with their rowing. And I, by my song, charmed the lofty rocks.[55] They receded in turn, and a wave rushed in with a loud sound. The rocks permitted the ship to pass and yielded to my cithara on account of my divine song. While singing my song, we escaped through a narrow channel between the Cyanae, and the rocks took root and stood motionless as though they

---

[54] So named for their blue color. These rocks are also called the Symplegades.

[55] Here Orpheus takes credit for an event attributed to Athena or Hera in earlier versions. In the traditional tale, the safe passage of the bird indicates the gods' promise that the Argo can pass safely through, though at the cost of its stern.

had always been fixed, for such had it been spun by Parca, the goddess of Fate.

Thus slipping away from bitter death, we avoided ruin on the Rhebas and the black beach. We passed then the long island of Thynias, near which the Tembrius full of fish becomes green and overflows its banks and the river Sangarius gushes waves into the Black Sea.

Lycus and the Back Sea

When we had rowed to the shore, we landed at the river Lycus. The ruler of the people there had the same name as the river, Lycus. He received the Minyan Heroes with a hospitable table, and he kept them in a friendly manner for several days and nights. There, fate brought death to two men: Idmon, son of Ampycus, and Tiphys the helmsman. The latter died of illness, while the former was killed by a wild boar in the countryside.

When we had built their tombs, we sailed under the trusted guidance of Ancaeus, for all said he was skilled in sailing and the best equipped with knowledge of the same. He took up the rudders in his hand, and steered the ship by the streams of Parthenius, which they call Callichorus. I made mention of this to you, Musaeus, in a lofty conversation. Sailing by the outer headland, we came near the land of the Paphlagonians.

Then the course of the Argo passed over into the great Black Sea. The ship reached Cape Carambis, in which the Thermodon[56] is situated,

---

[56] A river in northern Anatolia, on which the Amazons' capital was said to be situated.

and the streams of Halys, drawing the salty waves to the wide shore. Sailing lower down from the northern country for a little while, there was situated Themiscyra and Doeas, near which lie the cities of the Amazons. Also situated there, the Chalybes and Tibareni, neighboring peoples living mixed together in the region of the Mossyni.

Then sailing to the left, we put ashore where the Macrones border the Mariandyni. Further down, under Helix, a long neck of land was extended. In that place, resplendent ravines were surrounded by jutting ridges above a broad, curving bay. In that place stood the mount of Syme and a huge a verdant meadow. There was the stream of Araxes, the loud-sounding river, from which Thermodon, and Phasis, and Tanais flow, where there are the famous tribes of Colchi and Heniochi and Abasgi. We sailed, passing through the inmost harbors of the Ouri, Chindaei, Charandaei, and Solymi; the nation of the Assyrians and the uneven bends of Sinope; the Philyrae, Napatae, and the crowded towns of the Sapeires; and besides these, the Byzeres and the inhospitable Sigynnae.[57]

Arrival in Colchis

The Argo was carried through early in the morning by a blowing wind filling her sails, carried to the furthest ends of the Black Sea nearby the gently-flowing Phasis. Ancaeus exhorted everyone with his words to gather the sails and drop the yard

---

[57] A collection of traditional tribes largely derived from Apollonius' *Argonautica*, though arranged in a new order, perhaps, as Judith Bacon argued, due to corruption in the text.

and, with bent mast, sail forth by oars. After we entered the mouth of the gently flowing river, Ancaeus pointed out the strong walls of Aeëtes' fortified city, and the grove in which the Golden Fleece was suspended from an oak tree like hail.[58] In his heart and soul, Jason turned over his options, and he eloquently shared his question with the Minyans: whether to go alone to the house of Aeëtes and appease him by speaking gentle words, or whether to go with the Heroes and consider immediate battle?

It was not pleasing for all the Minyans to go, for the glorious goddess[59] had thrown fear and hesitation into their minds in order that she might meanwhile complete what divine will had ordained. Quickly, she commanded a vision of danger to occur in the house of Aeëtes. The dream quickly struck terrible fear in the heart of the king. He seemed to see on the lovely bosom of the young maiden Medea, whom he was raising in his halls, a glistening star darting across its heavenly path, which she, having taken it up on her robe, brought to water of the fair-flowing Phasis. He saw the star seize the maiden and carry her across the Black Sea. He suddenly woke up from this deceptive vision, and terrible fear dragged around his chest. Jumping up, he ordered his slaves to quickly prepare his horses to be yoked to his chariot to carry him to the beloved stream in order to placate the Nymphs and the souls of the heroes, however many would be wandering to the river.

So that they could be guarded, he called forth his perfumed daughters from their bedrooms: Chalciope with the sons of murdered

---

[58] The location of the Golden Fleece varies greatly by author. Here, the Fleece hangs in a sacred grove enclosed by walls. In Diodorus Siculus (4.47.1), the Fleece hangs in a temple of Ares, and it has been suggested that in early versions of the myth, such as that given in the now-fragmentary *Naupactia*, the Fleece's first location was within Aeëtes palace itself.

[59] Hera, Jason's special protector.

Phrixus,[60] and also tender Medea, gifted with excellent form, a chaste maiden. Absyrtus[61] lived away from the city in a separate dwelling.

Aeëtes got up into a gold chariot with his daughters, whom the horses swiftly carried through the plain and through the river bank full of reeds, to the place where they always made holy offerings and prayers to the river. The Argo came up to this very bank. Aeëtes gazed upon it, and he saw thereafter many seated Heroes resembling the immortals and clad in shining armor. But noble Jason stood out as the most handsome of all. Hera honored him in every way, giving him surpassing beauty, stature, and manliness. But when they gazed into each other's eyes, Aeëtes and the Minyans equally stiffened their chests. Aeëtes in his chariot and lustrous golden robes shone like the sun.[62] Ringing his head was a crown fringed with glowing rays. He swung with his hands a scepter like lightning. At his sides stood his two daughters, by whom he was made happy and triumphant. Thus approaching the ship and gazing with terrible eyes, he sent out a roaring voice from his chest, making horrendous threats and resounding loudly:

"Tell me who you are, what need sent you here, and from where. What makes you wish to cross the land of Cytae? Do you not dread my power or the people of Colchis, who bend to my scepter, well-skilled in battle and impervious even to the spear of Ares himself?"

Thus he spoke, but indeed the Argonauts gaped at him in silent astonishment. Therefore, Hera, the adored goddess, placed courage in the son of Aeson's breast. He roared back:

---

[60] Phrixus brought the Golden Fleece to Colchis and married Aeëtes' daughter. In this version he was murdered because an oracle said one of the family of Athamas, Phrixus' father, would overthrow Aeëtes. In other versions, he dies in Colchis of old age.

[61] Aeëtes' son, also called Aegialeus (e.g., Diodorus Siculus 4.45.3).

[62] Aeëtes and his sister Circe, children of the sun god Helios, shared his solar symbols.

"Neither did we come as bandits, nor did we undertake to wander from a foreign land to make abusive injury to men for the sake of advantage in life. In truth, my uncle Pelias, son of Poseidon, imposed this labor upon me, so that unless we take the Golden Fleece, we cannot return to Iolcus. Nor are my beloved companions ignoble. Some are children of gods, others of Heroes, unskilled neither in combat nor in battle. But we wish to be guests of your house. For this is better." Thus he spoke.

The soul of stormy Aeëtes was excited, weaving a dread trick against the heroes. After a long interval, he carried on a great conversation with the Minyans. "If indeed you will enter battle against the warlike Colchis and finish off its army of men, then without controversy the prize will be yours: You can take the fleece and return with it to your homeland. But if you leave even a few phalanxes, then this will be your prize: your death and the destruction of your ship. However, if you obey me, which is much more useful, then choose the most excellent among you and the most deserving of royal power. Him I will test with labors which I will dictate, and should he complete them, he will take away the Golden Fleece. That will be your prize." Thus speaking, he spurred on his horses, which carried him back.

Truly, grief seized the Minyans' souls. Then indeed the regret for the loss of Heracles moved over them; for without him they had no hope of defeating the invincible people of Colchis and reckless Ares.

*   *   *

Achievement of the Fleece

Now I will describe to you, O Musaeus, everything the Minyans did and suffered: Argus, one of the bellicose sons of Phrixus whom Chalciope bore (for she had been married to their father), came running back from the house of Aeëtes, announcing to the Minyans that Aeëtes had committed a pernicious crime against them. Then, on the advice of Hera, Medea of the unlucky marriage was conquered by the allure of Jason; for the Cytheran mother of love, Aphrodite, sent desire into her, and the most ancient one[63] sent an arrow into her heart. Then, Jason set two fire-breathing bulls under the yoke, planting four acres with seed that pugnacious Phrixus had brought with him when he came to Aeëtes' house: a dowry of the teeth of the dragon of Ares.[64] Jason killed the crop of hostile Spartoi by causing them to cut each other down, and the son of Aeson brought back splendid glory.

The maiden of the unlucky marriage came secretly from the house, wrapped in a robe as black as night. Her love and womanly need drove her on, so Medea came to the Argo, not worrying about keeping back her father's rage. She was embraced passionately by Jason and kissed furiously across her beautiful face, tears overflowing her cheeks. Nor did she have any of her favorite Hero's shame, and with acts of love she abandoned her maidenhood and her desire for an honest marriage.

---

[63] Eros.

[64] These were the teeth of the dragon slain by Cadmus, which when planted grew into armed men, the Spartoi. Here Phrixus brought them to Colchis as a marriage dowry, but it is usually said that Athena divided the teeth between Cadmus and Aeëtes.

Now you will hear of many other things.

When Medea had come from the house of Aeëtes in secret and arrived at our ship, we deliberated in our souls how best to approach and carry back the Golden Fleece from its sacred oak. We hoped this would be easy to do, for none of us knew this undertaking was hopeless. For great was the deed pressing down on all Heroes, and the deepest chasm of our troubles appeared. For before the house of Aeëtes and a rushing river, a fifty-four foot high enclosure stood before us, defended by towers and polished blocks of iron, crowned by seven defensive walls in a circle. Within it were three gigantic gates of bronze, between which ran a wall, and atop this, golden battlements. At one of the gateposts there stood the far-seeing queen, scattering with her motion the radiance of fire, whom the Colchians propitiate as Artemis of the gate,[65] resounding with the chase, terrible for men to see, and terrible to hear, unless one approaches by the sacred rites and purification, the rites kept hidden by the priestess who was initiated, Medea, unfortunate in marriage, along with the girls of Cyta. No mortal, whether native or stranger, entered that way, crossing over the threshold, for the terrible Goddess kept them away by all means, breathing madness into her fire-eyed dogs.

In the innermost recess of the enclosure was a sacred grove, shaded by green trees. Therein were many laurels, cornels, tall shoots, and grass, within which grew short plants with powerful roots: asphodel, beautiful maidenhair, rushes, galingale, delicate verbena, sage, hedge-mustard, purple honeysuckle, healing cassidony, flourishing field basil, mandrake, hulwort; in addition fluffy dittany, fragrant saffron, nose-smart; and also lion-foot, greenbrier, chamomile, black poppy, alcua, all-heal, white

---

[65] Orpheus is describing a statue or automaton atop the wall.

Figure 5. Diana and Hecate. This seventeenth-century illustration by Wenzel Hollar shows Artemis (the Roman Diana), the goddess of the hunt, and her dread counterpart, Hecate, sometimes said to be the same goddess. (Wikimedia Commons.)

hellebore, aconite, and other noxious plants which are born from the earth.[66] In the middle, the trunk of a great oak reached high, and the tree's branches overspread the grove. On this, spread over a long branch, hung the Golden Fleece, over which a terrible snake continuously watched, a serpent dangerous to men and indescribable. It was covered in golden scales and wound about the tree trunk with its huge coils, watching over the tomb of Zeus Chamaizelos[67] while guarding the

---

[66] These plants were associated with magic, necromancy, and healing. Such a collection of plants in Late Antiquity could be either a garden for medicine or magic.

[67] Earth-bound or chthonic Zeus (literally, "zealous for ground," an adjective used to describe plants that trail across the ground). The god had an infernal aspect sometimes identified with Hades, the Underworld god, who was also known as the "Other Zeus."

Fleece. Untiring, exempt from sleep, it kept guard over its charges, casting its gray eyes all about.

But when we heard the truth about Mounychian Hecate[68] and the guardian of the snake, for Medea had carefully explained this, we sought an unexpected way to accomplish the wretched undertaking: by placating savage Artemis so that we could appease the wild monster so we could steal the Fleece and return to our homeland. Then Mopsus, who knew of these things by his prophetic art, urged the other Heroes to beseech me and to thrust upon me the job of placating Artemis and soothing the monstrous beast. Thus, standing around me, they begged. I ordered to come with me to the place of the undertaking the son of Aeson; two strong men, Castor the horseman and Polydeuces the boxer; and Mopsus, son of Ampyx. Alone among the others, Medea followed me.

After I came to the enclosures and the sacred place, I dug a three-sided pit in some flat ground.[69] I quickly brought some trunks of juniper, dry cedar, prickly boxthorn and weeping black poplars, and in the pit I made a pyre of them. Skilled Medea brought to me many drugs, taking them from the innermost part of a chest smelling of incense. At once, I fashioned certain images from barley-meal.[70] I threw them onto the pyre, and as a sacrifice to honor the dead, I killed three black puppies. I mixed with their blood copper sulfate, soapwort, a sprig of safflower, and in addition odorless fleawort, red alkanet, and bronze-plant. After this, I filled the bellies of the puppies with this mixture and placed them

---

[68] Orpheus here identifies Artemis with dread Hecate, the underworld goddess of gates and magic. The two were often worshipped together or identified with one another.

[69] This ritual parallels the rite used by Jason to become invulnerable to the fire-breathing bulls in Apollonius' *Argonautica* (3.1191ff.). Both rites have necromantic overtones.

[70] The text is corrupt here.

on the wood. Then I mixed the bowels with water and poured the mixture around the pit. Dressed in a black mantle, I sounded bronze cymbals and made my prayer to the Furies. They heard me quickly, and breaking forth from the caverns of the gloomy abyss, Tisiphone, Allecto, and divine Megaira arrived, brandishing the light of death in their dry pine torches.

Suddenly the pit blazed up, and the deadly fire crackled, and the unclean flame sent high its smoke. At once, on the far side of the fire, the terrible, fearful, savage goddesses arose. One had a body of iron. The mortal call her Pandora.[71] With her came one who takes on various shapes, having three heads, a deadly monster you do not wish to know: Hecate of Tartarus. From her left shoulder leapt a horse with a long mane. On her right shoulder there could be seen a dog with a maddened face. The middle head had the shape of a lion[72] of wild form. In her hand she held a well-hilted sword. Pandora and Hecate circled the pit, moving this way and that, and the Furies leapt with them. Suddenly the wooden guardian statue of Artemis dropped its torches from its hands and raised its eyes to heaven. Her canine companions fawned. The bolts of the silver bars were loosened, the beautiful gates of the thick walls opened, and the sacred grove within came into view.

I crossed the threshold. Then Medea, the daughter of Aeëtes, and the glorious son of Aeson, and the Tyndarids[73] at the same time pressed in, followed by Mopsus. But when we could see nearby the lovely oak and the pedestal and altar base of chthonic Zeus, then the snake lifted

---

[71] The first woman and the cause of all suffering (Hesiod *Theogony* 590-3; *Works and Days* 60-105). This figure may derive from an earlier goddess of the earth, suggested in the scholia to Aristophanes' *The Birds* (ad 971).

[72] Some texts give this head as a snake instead.

[73] Castor and Polydeuces, the sons of Tyndarus.

Figure 6. Jason and Medea. Jason seizes the Golden Fleece from the sleeping serpent as Medea watches. Fragment of a second century CE Roman sarcophagus, now in the National Museum of Rome. (© Marie-Lan Nguyen/Wikimedia Commons. Used under Creative Commons license.)

his head and fearsome jaws from beneath his broad coils and let out a deadly hiss. The boundless ether roared; the trees resounded, shaking from their tips to their roots. The shaded grove cried out. In truth, trembling seized me and my companions. Alone among us, Medea kept in her breast a fearless soul: for she had pulled up with her hands deadly roots. Then I matched my divine voice with my tortoise-shell lyre, resounding deeply, plucking its lowest-pitched string. I called upon Sleep, king of the gods and all men, to come and beguile the might of the immense snake. Yielding to me at once, he came to the land of Cyta, on his way putting to sleep tribes of men weary from the day's work, powerful blasts of winds, waves of the sea, springs of ever-flowing water, gliding rivers, beasts and birds, and everything living and moving he persuaded to sleep under his golden wings. Thus he came to the blooming land of the harsh Colchians. A deep sleep suddenly settled on the serpent's eyes, the likeness of death. He laid out his long neck, his head weighed down by his scales.

The unfortunate Medea was struck dumb seeing this. Encouraging the glorious son of Aeson, she impelled him to quickly seize the Golden Fleece from the tree. He did not refuse her command, but took away the vast Fleece and came to the ship. The Minyan heroes were exceedingly glad and lifted their hands to the immortals living in the wide heaven. Thus they gazed upon the Fleece.

Murder of Absyrtus; Northward Journey

Soon Aeëtes heard from a slave-girl that Medea had departed. He enjoined Absyrtus to call together the people and to search for the girl, his sister. The swift Absyrtus hurried to the river bank, to the crowd of Heroes, and discovered there the dread maiden. Night had cut a middle path through the star-spangled sky when, through a hateful fraud, Absyrtus, who was pursuing the wife of Jason, was killed and cut down on account of Medea's deadly love. Therefore, the Argonauts threw down the murdered man onto the banks and into the mouth of the rushing river. By a strong wind pushing a wave across the sterile sea, Absyrtus' body was drawn to a set of islands which are therefore called the Absyrtides.[74] This did not escape the watchful gaze of Zeus, or his divine will.

When they had recovered themselves within the ship and they had cut themselves free from the shore, spurred on by quick rowing, they traversed the river. By no means, however, could we travel to the fish-filled Black Sea by the direct path through the wide mouth of the Phasis, but we were forced to wander much in sailing back.

The cities of the Colchians were left behind by the unsuspecting Minyans. Enveloped by darkness, but pressing on with our oars, we unknowingly hurried up the river, running through the middle of a plain. There men living on both sides were: the Gymni, Buonomae, and the rustic Arkyes; and the Cercetici and the ferocious Sinti, who established their seat in the middle of the surrounding Charandaei, near the headland of the Caucasus by the strait of Erytheia. But when there appeared the newborn dawn, pleasing to men, we landed at a grassy island. There two rivers split their courses: the wide Phasis flowing with un-navigable waves, and the placidly flowing Saranges, which gushes forth with a roar into Lake Maeotis[75] through marshy grasses. Rowing, we sailed a night and a day, and after three quarters of two more[76] we came to the Bosporus[77] between the Marsh[78] and the Black Sea, where once the

---

[74] The Absyrtides were traditionally identified with islands at the head of the Adriatic, where Apollonius had Absyrtus killed, but appear here in the Black Sea.

[75] Identified usually as the Sea of Azov but possibly also with the Caspian Sea.

[76] I.e., thirty-six hours.

[77] The Cimmerian Bosporus, now the Strait of Kerch, separating the Sea of Azov from the Black Sea.

[78] I.e., Lake Maeotis, famous for the marshes surrounding the mouth of the Don.

cattle-stealing Titan,[79] sitting upon a strong bull, divided the passage from the swampy lake.

Weary from an entire day of rowing, we arrived[80] first at the softly-robed tribe of the Maetoae, and then the Geloni and the long-haired Bathyagri, and the Getae, and the Gymnaei[81] and Cecryphes, and the Arsopes and Arimaspi, peoples rich in cattle, of whom a tribe was living near the lake of Maeotis. For when the Immortals threw forth great trouble, we transfixed the outer waters of a raging whirlpool, which carried us away. There the water is confined by the low banks of the swamp, driven up with a great crashing sound, from where a great forest resounded, at the northern limits of the Ocean. And blown past, the Argo proceeded through the mouth of the river.

Working nine nights and as many days, we left behind here and there countless savage nations: the Pacti, the Arctei, and the proud Lelii;[82] the Scythians armed with arrows, faithfully serving Ares; and the Tauri, who offer gloomy sacrifices to Mounychia,[83] their mixing bowl moistened with human blood. We travelled past the Hyperboreans,[84] the Nomads, and the Caspians. But after the tenth birth of Dawn, who brings light to men, we landed at the Rhipaean hills.

---

[79] Possibly Heracles, who is called a Titan in the Orphic Hymn to him (No. 12). The myth to which this passage refers does not survive.

[80] From this point, the geography of the poem becomes confused and tribes of varying degrees of historical reality are discussed. The Maeotae, Geloni, Sauromatae, Getae, Gymnaei (Hylaei) and Arimaspi are attested in other ancient sources. The Bathyagri, Cecryphes, and Arsopes are not. These tribes are placed very roughly in their historical locations, though the Geloni are too far south, and the Getae and Hylaei too far east.

[81] Some scholars have amended this to read Hylaei, a better-attested tribal name.

[82] These tribes are unknown and may be entirely fictional.

[83] Artemis. The Tauri of the Crimea were said to worship the goddess with human sacrifices of shipwrecked travelers and captured Greeks (Herodotus, *Histories* 4.103).

[84] A people living beyond the land of Boreas. Since Boreas' home was Thrace, this could refer to any land to the north, possibly Eastern Europe, or even Scandinavia.

From here, the Argo made advances by leaps and jumps through the narrow strait, and fell into the Ocean, which the Hyperborean men call the Cronian Sea or the Dead Sea.[85] We did not trust that it would be possible to escape sad ruin, had not Ancaeus, pressing hard upon the polished rudders with the greatest fury, righted the charging ship so that it would go along the right-hand shore. He pushed the ship forward, driving on the rudders with both hands. But after laborious rowing, the Argonauts' exhausted hands did not remain on duty, but with a sad heart they supported their heads with their hands, wishing for sweat to make them cool. Meanwhile, they burned with hunger.

Ancaeus sprung up and roused all the other Heroes, speaking to them with gentle words. Then coming up to tenacious mud in the sea, they sent their feet over the walls of the ship and at once descended from her on twisted ropes. Ancaeus and Argus threw a long rope from the stern, and catching the end, they gave it to the Heroes, who at once hurried to the shore, straining to drag the seafaring ship. And thus the ship followed where they drew her, along the clear way across the polished pebbles of the shore, for no blowing breeze stirred that low sea, where Helix is and the farthest wave of Tethys.

When six dawns had come, we reached the happy and rich Macrobii,[86] who live for many healthy years, twelve thousand months corresponding to hundreds of years of the full moon, free from all troubles of age. But after they finish the fated number of months, they take hold of a pleasant end by dying in their sleep. Meanwhile, the life of a man is free from care, thoughts of food, or toil. They graze on pastures

---

[85] The North Sea or Arctic Ocean, though Apollonius placed it in the Adriatic.

[86] Confusingly, the Macrobii of Orpheus appear to match the description of the Hyperboreans in Pliny (*Natural History* 4.26) and Pindar (*Pythian* 10).

with plants sweetened with honey, drinking the powerful dew of divine ambrosia.[87] Tranquility they always experience, a placid serenity across eyes and brows. Their just temperament resides in both children and parents, in both their minds and souls, endowing them with eloquent wisdom and just speaking. We traveled through here, pressing the shore with our feet.

Pulling the swift ship, we then came to the Cimmerians, who are without the splendid light of the sun. For the Rhipaean mountains and the Calpius block the rising sun and shut out brightness. Phlegra overshadows the noontime sun, and the sharp-peaked Alps block the evening light.[88] So the Cimmerians are always in darkness.[89] When we once again went forth, pushing the ship with our feet, we came to a rough headland and a river devoid of wind, where a gushing river rushed forth from a deep whirlpool, gold-bearing Acheron, through a cold region, rolling water of glittering silver. A black marsh kept it back, and the green trees next to the river's shores made a loud noise, always weighed down night and day with fruit. Next to this low pasture was found Hermioneia,[90] with defensive walls running around well-built villages. In this there lived the most just tribe of men, for whom transport by a single

---

[87] The food of the gods, conveying immortality.

[88] The geography here is particularly obscure. These geographic features are unknown, though possibly they originally referred to a region in Pannonia, according to the analysis of Judith Bacon ("The Geography of the *Orphic Argonautica*," *The Classical Quarterly* 25, nos. 3-4 [1931]: 181).

[89] The origins of this tale seem to lie in Homer, who had a (possibly unrelated) tribe of Cimmerians living in perpetual darkness at the edge of the world, near the gate to Hades (*Odyssey* 11.14ff.).

[90] This place is sometimes identified with an island near Britain. Scholars, however, suggest that its origin lies in a distorted version of Hermion in the Argolid. This city was located near two fabled entrances to Hades, as well as sanctuaries of Demeter and Persephone and an island of pines, just as the Argonauts found upon leaving Hermioneia (Bacon, "Geography," 181).

ship alone suffices after death: for their souls cross over the Acheron from the city by ship immediately. Near this are cities, unconquered gates to Hades, and the land of phantoms.

The Argo Speaks; the Island of Demeter

Afterward, we passed by both cities and homes, suffering by our misfortune a grave disaster. Ancaeus entered the ship, and at once he ordered all the crew to take their seats, and he spoke to us with flattering words: "Endure this labor, friends, because I hope no worse will arise for us. For I now see a rising Zephyr bristling up. Not without reason does the water of Ocean make noise against the sands. But quickly raise the mast and loosen the sails from the rope! Bringing the rope, quickly tie together the sails on both sides of the ship!" And each took pains to do so. And from the belly of the ship, a bellow sounded from the beech beam of Tomaros,[91] which when the Argo was constructed Pallas had built into it. In truth, entering our dumb-struck minds, it said:

"Ah! Woe! If only I had been destroyed by the Cyanae in the Inhospitable Sea, never having to hear of the crime of the good king I carry. Since now Erinys[92] follows closely behind us, seeking murdered Absyrtus. Disaster and calamity hem us in. She will punish the cause of this deadly and sad crime when I first come near the Isle of Ierne.[93]

---

[91] The mountain overlooking Dodona, where the talking beam was cut.
[92] One of the Furies, personifying wrath.
[93] This island is frequently identified with Ireland.

Pressing me to the Sacred Headland you need to direct the ship within the curve of the earth, or you will run out into the Atlantic Ocean." Thus the voice of fate fell silent.

But the inner mind of the Minyans was stupefied. Accordingly, they had cause to fear that due to Jason's love, death and disaster awaited. And they began to consider with bitter souls whether to kill Medea of the unfortunate marriage and throw her overboard as a prize for the fishes. Would this turn away Erinys? And they would have done so, had not the noble son of Aeson quickly realized what they were about to do and, humbly beseeching them, settled their souls. Moreover, they sat down at their oars after hearing the truthful voice of Argus, and quickly they took hold of the oars. Ancaeus skillfully held the rudders, and sailing by the island of Ierne, a fierce dark storm bellowing behind, the sails billowed out and the ship quickly ran through the clear waves. No one hoped any longer for escape from certain ruin.

The dawn had now come twelve times, and not a single man would have known within his soul where we were, had not Lynceus recognized the tranquil far shore of the river Ocean. For he caught sight from afar of a pine-covered island and the great houses of the Queen Demeter, surrounded by a black cloud. Of this story, intelligent Musaeus, you have heard: how once, Persephone's sisters led her through a great and wide wood, holding in her hands plucked flowers, and how Plouton approached the girl with his black horses by permission of Zeus and seized her and carried her through the barren waves.[94]

Then I abandoned any hope of sailing along the shore and those gleaming houses, where no man had come by ship. The harbor offers no

---

[94] This is the rape of Persephone by Hades (Plouton), told in the *Homeric Hymn to Demeter*, which led to Persephone becoming the queen of the Underworld.

safety for ships but a tall and precipitous rock encircles all. Nor was the helmsman of the unlucky ship, Ancaeus, without faith in me, but at once he drove to change course backward, bending the helm to the left. Thus doing, he proceeded on the proper path, but the current dragged us toward the right.

Circe and the Pillars of Heracles

On the third day we came to the house of Circe, to the Lycaean shore, and the sea surrounding its residences. We approached the beach, and we bound the ship to the shore with rocks. Jason sent beloved crewmen from the ship to go and inquire as to what kind of men lived in this great land and to learn about their cities and the settlements of their people. But suddenly there arrived the maiden sister of noble Aeëtes, a daughter of Helios (whom they call Circe, whose mother was Asterope and her father far-shining Hyperion[95]). She quickly came down to the ship. All were struck dumb by this sight. From her head hung hair like rays of light. Her beautiful face shone out, and her breath grew bright with flames. With her eye she caught sight of Medea, wrapped in a garment (as though the veil would cover her pallor and her shame, and the aching of her heart). Feeling pity for her, she spoke to her with these words:

"Oh unfortunate, unfortunate one! What terrible fate has Cypris thrust upon you? It does not escape me that you come to my island polluted with your crime against your old father and your brother,

---

[95] Helios, the sun.

whom I am astounded to adduce you killed. Therefore I adjudge that you shall not return to your native shores until you atone for this crime. You will wash yourself clean of the crime on the shores of Maleia[96] with Orpheus' knowledge of divine expiation. You may not enter my house by divine law, for you are contaminated by a crime of great magnitude. Meanwhile, I will at once send you gifts from host to guest in a spirit of goodwill: bread, sweet unmixed wine, and also much meat." Thus speaking, she flew back. Indeed, food and drink were prepared and set in the ship.

A strong favorable wind arose and sent us on our course. Then we loosened the ship from the island, and we came through the mouth of Tartessus, and we approached the Pillars of Heracles,[97] and we completed our circuit around the sacred headland of King Bacchus by night, when our soul was in need of sustenance.

Charybdis and the Sirens

When the dawn had brought light from the east, early in the morning we cleaved the sea with our oars. We came to Sardinia in the sea, and the bay of the Latins, and we were carried to the shores of the Ausonian[98] islands. Afterward, we held the sounding sea by Lilybaeum, and we moved along the three-sided

---

[96] On the southern tip of the Peloponnesus, known for its proverbial heavy wind.

[97] The Strait of Gibraltar.

[98] I.e., the islands of the Italian coast, such as Capri, so named for the Ausones, an Italic tribe. Here, however, the poet seems to include Corsica and Sardinia as Ausonian isles.

island,[99] the flames of Mount Etna trying to hold us back. Over the prow dangerous waves boiled up from the deep, and with hissing from the innermost chasm, Charybdis stirred up the greatest evil with churning waves. But the wave, reversing itself in turn, held the ship back in the same place, able to go neither forward nor back, but compelled to circle around the raging abyss. The Argo would surely have been submerged in the depths had not the powerful daughter born to the Old Man of the Sea,[100] Thetis, wanted to see her husband Peleus again. She rose from the depths and freed the Argo from ruin, and guarded her from the churning sea.

Then while sailing along, we saw not very far off a rocky headland. A steep cliff overhung a lofty and projecting rock, eaten into deep caverns within which the dark waves resounded terribly. Here we happened to meet girls who sang with a melodious voice, charming the ears of men so that they would forget returning home. The Minyans listened enraptured to the Sirens' song. They did not want to sail on past the dangerous voice, and they dropped the oars from their hands. Ancaeus steered straight for the headland. I grabbed my lyre and sang a glorious song my mother taught me. I sang a melodious song with my divine voice while plucking my lyre, a song of how long ago a quarrel over the swiftest of horses arose between Zeus, thundering from on high, and Poseidon, shaking land and sea. The blue god Poseidon, angry at Father Zeus, struck the land of Lycaonia with his golden trident and spread its broken pieces across the immense sea, so that it was no longer a mainland but rather three islands surrounded by sea. These are called Euboea, Sardinia, and windy Cyprus. Thus singing with my cithara, upon

---

[99] Sicily.

[100] The Titan Nereus, said to live in the Aegean Sea.

the snowy rock the Sirens were struck dumb, and they stopped their song. One dropped her flute; another dropped her tortoise-shell lyre from her hands. They groaned deeply since they had come to their sad fate and their destined death.[101] They threw themselves headlong from the heights down to the depths of the unquiet sea, in which their bodies and distinguished forms were changed into rocks.

Alcinous and the Marriage of Jason and Medea

Even after evading this fate, swift Argo finished her passage through wave and bending sea, and the wind, blowing against the forestay and the stern, drove us to divine Corcyra, where lived a race of skilled oarsman and seafarers, the Phaeacians. They were given their laws by the command of their most just king, Alcinous. Therefore, we prepared to land to make sacrifices to All-Seeing Zeus and the Apollo of the shores. But rowing fast, there came innumerable ships, a powerful fleet sent by Aeëtes: Colchians, Erravi, Charandaei, and Solymi.[102] They were looking for the Minyans so that they could lead Medea back to her distinguished father Aeëtes to be punished for the crime of killing her brother. When they had come to the harbor, at once heralds went forth to Alcinous.

---

[101] In some versions of the Sirens' myth, they were fated to die if anyone heard their song and lived. Here the poet differs from Homer's account where it was Odysseus, not the Argonauts, who cause the Sirens' death (*Odyssey* 12.39 ff. and 166ff.). In Apollonius (*Argonautica* 4.891-919), the scene plays out much the same as the Argonauts pass, but the Sirens do not die out of respect for Homeric precedent.

[102] Tribes of the Black Sea coast, here depicted as subject to or allied with Colchis.

Medea trembled with fear, and terror corrupted her noble visage, lest the Phaeacian king send her back unwillingly to her home and they destroy her as an example. The goddess Parca[103] had not yet fixed her will, not until the house of Pelias was destroyed and Jason himself brought an evil death to the king. But when Arete, forearms decorated with roses, and Alcinous, like unto a god, heard the cruel command of King Aeëtes, Alcinous at once allowed the armed ships to lead the girl away so that she could receive her punishment. The famous Queen Arete felt sympathy for Medea and coaxed her husband, speaking thusly:

"It is not pleasing to break a marriage, to disturb the nuptial bed, to extinguish the torch of love. Dionaean Aphrodite[104] will become violently angry at the man or woman who undertakes such an effort. Indeed, if Medea is a virgin and came here sexually intact, she should depart for her homeland in Colchis. But if she is sexually experienced and lost her virginity in the marital bed, her husband should take her away." Thus said she.

Alcinous absorbed this speech in his soul, and ordered that everything should be done as the queen had said. And this decision did not escape the Minyans, for at once Hera, making her body look like that of a slave, flew into the ship. She quickly reported what the king and queen had decided, and she indicated what they needed to do. Then Medea prepared a marriage bed on the highest part of the stern. The crew spread a matting of rushes. They spread out the Golden Fleece itself, and then they suspended from spears the hide of a bull and shields. And so they hid for modesty's sake the act of marriage. Then Medea of

---

[103] One of the Fates

[104] Aphrodite was the daughter of Dione (Homer, *Iliad* 5.370ff.).

the unlucky marriage was deprived of the flower of a girl's maidenhood, un-praised by wedding hymns.

Afterward, Colchians and Minyans came in view of the king and queen, and they pleaded their cause. The son of Aeson accepted the judgment of Alcinous, and he led away his wife Medea with him. At once the Argonauts loosened the ship's oars, and rowing with many conversations, the Argo ran ahead, cleaving the Ambracian Gulf.

Crete and the Return Home

Now, Museaus, born of a goddess, I will relate to you all that the Minyans suffered after this, from the winds around Syrtis and how they were protected on their wandering voyage over the sea. We suffered a great enemy on Crete, when we observed a bronze giant[105] who allowed no one to go into the harbor. And so, driven back into a narrow passage by the low echo of a sea wave, we suddenly feared being covered by a black tempest lest we be dashed upon the gloomy and forbidding rocks. But from nearby, far-throwing Paean[106] heard our cries. He shot a dart from rocky Delos and revealed himself in the middle of the Sporades on the island which all the neighboring peoples called Anaphe.

But it was not divine law that the son of Aeson should be prevented from sailing the sea, for he brought his atonement with him. The dangerous Fate, Parca, recoiled. (Not without cause was Hyperion angry.)

---

[105] Talos, the bronze man created by Hephaestus to protect Crete.
[106] An epithet of Apollo as the god of healing.

Figure 7. Talos armed with a stone. Obverse of a silver didrachm of Phaistos, Crete, c. 300 BCE. (Public domain image, Marie-Lan Nguyen/Wikimedia Commons.)

We rowed to the farthest shore of Maleia, where Circe had advised, to avert the curses of Aeëtes and calm the persecuting fury of Erinys. I made expiatory sacrifices for the Minyans, and I prayed to Poseidon, the god who shakes the earth, that he might permit our safe return, and allow us the sight of our native land, and bless the Minyans with the embraces of their beloved parents.

And indeed the Minyans pressed on, sailing to the well-cultivated Iolcus; and I approached windy Taenaron, making an offering to the celebrated kings who hold the keys to the underworld abyss. Thus quickly departing, I pressed on to snowy Thrace, in the region of the Libethrians,[107] in my homeland, entering the famous cave[108] where my mother gave birth to me on the bed of the brave Oeagrus.[109]

---

[107] The best-known Libethra, or Leibethra, was located near Mt. Olympus but was once populated, according to Strabo, by an ancient migration of Thracians. The Orphic poet here speaks of another Libethra, found in Thrace itself, in the region of the Odrysians. Both Libethras were associated with Orpheus, though the Olympian Libethra is traditionally the place of Orpheus' death and burial.

[108] This is traditionally a cave near Pimplea beside Mount Olympus, but here the poet has transferred the scene to Thrace, where a cave of the Nymphs traditionally associated with Orpheus was found on Mount Helicon near Libethra.

[109] The father of Orpheus, and a king of Thrace. Despite hailing from Thrace, Apollonius has Oeagrus marry Calliope at Pimplea (*Argonautica* 1.23ff.). The Orphic poet appears to speak instead of a tradition that located the events of Orpheus' life in Thrace.

Part Two
SELECTED ROMAN AND MEDIEVAL WRITERS ON THE VOYAGE OF THE ARGONAUTS

Gaius Julius Hyginus lived in Roman Spain in the first century CE. Hyginus was a freedman of Caesar Augustus, who appointed him superintendent of the Palatine Library. It is likely that Hyginus wrote at least two treatises on mythology, including a retelling of the stories of gods and heroes and another on astronomical lore, both drawing on valuable Greek sources now lost to us. Neither survives in its original form. Instead, under the name of Hyginus, we possess two sets of what appear to be a schoolboy's notes abbreviating his treatises. The *Fabulae* (Fables), from which the following passages have been drawn, have long been recognized as being poor in quality and writing style; however, this work is important for preserving variant myths recorded nowhere else.

The Fabulae of Hyginus
(3, 12-25)

3. Phrixus

When Phrixus and Helle[1] were wandering through a forest while possessed by madness sent by Liber,[2] their mother Nebula is said to have come there with a Golden Ram, whose parents were Neptune[3] and Theophane, and to have ordered them to mount the ram and travel to Colchis and King Aeëtes, son of Sol, and there sacrifice the ram to Mars. They were said to have done this, but when they had mounted and the ram had carried them over the open sea, Helle fell off the ram, and from this the sea is named Hellespont. But Phrixus was conveyed to Colchis; where, as his mother had ordered, he sacrificed the ram and set up in the temple of Mars its fleece, which it is said Jason, son of Aeson and Alcimede, came to take. But Aeëtes freely took in Phrixus and gave his daughter Chalciope as a wife; and afterward she bore children unto him. But Aeëtes feared they would expel him from his kingdom because he had received warnings from portents to beware of death from a foreigner, a son of Aeolus; and

---

[1] The events described in Fabula 3 are the background for the Argonauts' story, explaining how the Golden Fleece came to Colchis. Fabula 2 explains the reasons behind this. Ino, the stepmother of Phrixus and Helle, wished them dead to solidify her position with her husband Athamas, so she contrived to frame Phrixus for the destruction of the harvest by contriving a fake oracular response calling for his sacrifice.

[2] The Roman deity of wine, freedom, and fertility.

[3] Hyginus wrote in Latin, so the gods are given by their Roman names.

so he killed Phrixus. But his[4] sons Argus, Phrontis, Melas, and Cylindrus embarked on a ship to go to their grandfather Athamas. While on his quest for the Fleece, Jason rescued the shipwrecked men from the island of Dia and carried them back to their mother Chalciope, by whose favor he was recommended to her sister Medea.

12. Pelias

It was told to Pelias, son of Cretheus and Tyro, that his death would approach if a monocrepis (that is, a man shod on only one foot) arrived while he was sacrificing to Neptune. While he made his annual sacrifice to Neptune, Jason, son of Aeson, brother of Pelias, desiring to make a sacrifice, lost his sandal while he crossed the river Evenus.[5] He did nothing about this in order to make it to the sacrifice quickly. When Pelias, observing this, recalled the prophesy he had received, he ordered him to ask his enemy King Aeëtes for the golden fleece of the ram which Phrixus had consecrated to Mars at Colchis. Calling together the leaders of Greece, he[6] set out for Colchis.

13. Juno

When Juno, near the river Evenus, had turned herself into an old woman and stood there to test men's minds to see if they would carry her across the river, and no one was willing, Jason, son of Aeson and Alcimede, carried her across. She, angry

---

[4] Phrixus.

[5] I.e., the river Anaurus.

[6] Jason.

at Pelias, who had omitted to make a sacrifice to her, caused Jason to leave behind one sandal in the mud.

14. Argonauts Assembled

Jason, son of Aeson and Alcymede, daughter of Clymene, leader of the Thessalians.

Orpheus, son of Oeagrus and the Muse Calliope, a Thracian from the city of Pieria, which is on Mount Olympus on the River Enipeus, prophet and cithara player.

Asterion, the son of Pyremus, mother Antigone, daughter of Pheres, from the city of Pellene. Others call him the son of Hyperasius, from the city of Piresia, which is at the base of Mt. Phylleus, which is in Thessaly, from which place two rivers, Apidanus and Epineus, flowing separately, join into one.

Polyphemus, son of Elatus, mother Hippea, daughter of Antippus, a Thessalian from the city of Larissa, with a limp foot.

Iphiclus, son of Phylacus, mother Periclymene, daughter of Minyas, from Thessaly, Jason's maternal uncle.

Admetus, son of Pheres, mother Periclymene, daughter of Minyas, from Thessaly, Mount Chalcodonius, from which both the town and river take their name. There Apollo pastured his flock.

Eurytus and Echion, sons of Mercury and Antianira, daughter of Menetus, from the city of Alope, which is now called Ephesus. Some authors think them Thessalians.

Aethalides, son of Mercury and Eupolemia, daughter of Myrmidon. He was Larissaean.

Coronus, son of Caenus, from the city of Gyrton, which is in Thessaly. This Caenus, son of Elatus, a Magnesian, demonstrated that in no way could Centaurs wound him with steel but only with tree trunks sharpened into points. Some say that he had been a woman who, because she served Neptune as one would in marriage, received a wish and was changed into a young man who could not be killed by anything. This has never been done, and it is not possible for any mortal to be unable to be killed by steel, or changed from a woman to a man.

Mopsus, son of Ampycus and Chloris, trained in augury by Apollo, came from Oechalia, or as some think was Titarensian.

Eurydamas, son of Irus and Demonassa. Others call him the son of Cteminus who lived in the city of Dolopeidem near Lake Xynius.

Theseus[7] son of Aegeus and Aethra, daughter of Pittheus, from Troezen; others say he was from Athens.

Pirithous, son of Ixion, brother of the Centaurs, a Thessalian.

Menoetius, son of Actor, an Opuntian.

Eriboetes, the son of Teleon, from Eleon.

Eurytion, son of Irus and Demonassa.

... ixition[8] from the town of Cerinthus.

Oileus, son of Hodoedocus and Agrianome, daughter of Perseon, from the city of Narycea.

Clyteus and Iphitus, sons of Eurytus and Antiope, daughter of Pylo, kings of Oechalia. Others say they came from Euboea. This Eurytus,

---

[7] Theseus is rarely numbered among the Argonauts. In Apollonius, he lived before Jason. In most other authors, he is a later figure, the stepson to Medea.

[8] The text is corrupt here. This may be a corruption of "ex Iton," from the town of Iton, followed by missing text giving the name of the man from Cerinthus, who can be restored from Apollonius of Rhodes (*Argonautica* 1.77-79) as Canthus. Thus, this line and the following would then read: "Eurytion, son of Irus and Demonassa, from Iton. Canthus, the son of Canethus, from the town of Cerinthus."

after receiving knowledge of archery from Apollo, is said to have contended with the granter of this gift. His son Clyteus was killed by Aeëtes.

Peleus and Telamon, sons of Aeacus and Endeis, daughter of Chiron, from the island of Aegina. Because they murdered their brother Phocus, they left behind their residence and sought new homes in different places: Peleus in Phthia, and Telamon Salamis, which Apollonius of Rhodes calls Atthis.

Butes, son of Teleon and Zeuxippe, daughter of the river Eridanus, from Athens.

Phalerus, son of Alcon, from Athens.

Tiphys, son of Phorbas and Hyrmine, a Boeotian; he was the helmsman for the ship Argo.

Argus, son of Polybus and Argia; others call him the son of Danaus. He was an Argive, and he covered himself in the hide of a young black-haired bull. He was the builder of the ship Argo.

Phliasus, son of Father Liber and Ariadne, daughter of Minos, from the city Phlius, which is in the Peloponnesus. Others call him a Theban.

Hylas, son of Theodamas and the nymph Menodice, daughter of Orion, a youth from Oechalia, others say from Argos, a companion of Hercules.

Nauplius, son of Neptune and Amymone, daughter of Danaus, an Argive.

Idmon, son of Apollo and the nymph Cyrene, some say of Abas, an Argive. He was skilled in augury, and though he realized he would die beforehand from birds who foretold it, he did not abandon the fatal campaign.

Castor and Pollux, sons of Jove and Leda, daughter of Thestius, Lacedaemonians; others call them Spartans, both beardless. It is written that at the same time stars appeared on their heads as if they had seemingly fallen there.

Lynceus and Idas, sons of Aphareus and Arena, daughter of Oebalus, Messenians from the Peloponnesus. They say that of these, Lynceus could see what was hidden underground, nor was he prevented by darkness. Others say Lynceus could see nothing at night. He was said to see underground because he knew gold mining. When he descended and was pointing out the gold, suddenly rumors spread that he could see beneath the earth. Likewise, Idas was vigorous and fierce.

Periclymenus, son of Neleus and Chloris, daughter of Amphion and Niobe; he was from Pylos.

Amphidamas and Cepheus, sons of Aleus and Cleobule, from Arcadia.

Ancaeus, son of Lycurgus; others say grandson, from Tegea.

Augeas, son of the Sun and Nausidame, daughter of Amphidamas; he was an Elean.

Asterion and Amphion, sons of Hyperasius, others say of Hippasus, from Pellene.

Euphemus, son of Neptune and Europe, daughter of Tityus, a Taenarian. It is said he was able to run over water with dry feet.

Another Ancaeus, son of Neptune by Althaea, daughter of Thestius, from the island Imbrasus, which was called Parthenia but is now called Samos.

Erginus, son of Neptune, from Miletus; some say of Periclymenus, from Orchomenus.

Meleager, son of Oeneus and Althaea, daughter of Thestius; some think (a son) of Mars, a Calydonian.

Laocoön, son of Porthaon, brother of Oeneus, a Calydonian.

Another Iphiclus, son of Thestius, mother Leucippe, brother of Althaea by the same mother, a Lacedaemonian; a swift runner and thrower of the javelin.

Iphitus, son of Naubolus, from Phocis; others say that he was the son of Hippasus from the Peloponnesus.

Zetes and Calaïs, sons of the wind Aquilo and Orithyia, daughter of Erechtheus. They were said to have had wings on their heads and feet, and dark blue locks of hair, and to have travelled through the air. They drove away the three birds called Harpies—Aëllopous, Celaeno, and Ocypete, daughters of Thaumas and Ozomene—from Phineus, son of Agenor, at the time when Jason's comrades were on their way to Colchis. They used to live on the Strophades Islands in the Aegean Sea, which are called the Plotae. They were said to be feathered and to have chickens' heads, wings, and human arms. However, Zetes and Calaïs were slain by Hercules' weapons.[9] The stones set up over their tombs are moved by their father's breath.[10] Moreover, they are said to be from Thrace.

Phocus and Priasus, sons of Caeneus, from Magnesia.

Eurymedon, son of Father Liber and Ariadne, daughter of Minos, from Phlius.

Palaemonius, son of Lernus, a Calydonian.

Actor, son of Hippasus, from the Peloponnesus.

Thersanon, son of the Sun and Leucothoe, from Andros.

Hippalcimus, son of Pelops and Hippodamia, daughter of Oenomaus, from the Peloponnesus, from Pisa.

---

[9] On the island of Tenos, supposedly in revenge for convincing the Argonauts to leave Hercules behind after the loss of Hylas.

[10] The tomb of the Boreads on Tenos was said to be marked with two funerary stelae, one of which moved when the north wind blew (Apollonius, *Argonautica* 1.1304-8).

Asclepius, son of Apollo and Coronis, from Tricca.

[Amphiaraus, son of Oecles, mother Hypermestra],[11] Thestius' daughter, an Argive.

Neleus, son of Hippocoon, from Pylos.

Iolaus, son of Iphiclus, an Argive.

Deucalion, son of Minos and Pasiphaë, daughter of Sol, from Crete.

Philoctetes, son of Poeas, from Meliboea.

Another Caeneus, son of Coronus, from Gortyn.

Acastus, son of Pelias and Anaxibia, daughter of Bias, from Iolcus, covered in a two-layered cloak. He joined the Argonauts as a volunteer, a companion of Jason of his own will.

Moreover, all these are called Minyae, either because the daughters of Minyas gave birth to them, or because Jason's mother was the daughter of Clymeste, the daughter of Minyas.

But neither did they all reach Colchis, nor all return to their homelands. For Hylas, in Moesia near Cios and the river Ascanius, was seized by Nymphs. When Hercules and Polyphemus were searching for him, they were left behind as a wind carried away the ship. Polyphemus was also left behind by Hercules, founded a city in Moesia, and died among the Chalybes. Moreover, Tiphys succumbed to illness among the Maryandini in Propontis at the house of King Lycus; in his place Ancaeus, son of Neptune, guided the ship to Colchis. Moreover, Idmon, son of Apollo, also died at the house of King Lycus; he was gored by a boar when he went out for straw.[12] The avenger of Idmon was Idas, son of Aphareus, who killed the boar. Butes, son of Teleon, although distracted by the singing and cithara-playing of Orpheus, nevertheless

---

[11] Missing text restored from Fabula 70.

[12] The text here is corrupt, perhaps originally "when he left the walls."

was overcome by the sweetness of the song of the Sirens, dove into the sea to swim to them. Venus saved him at Lilybaeum as the waves carried him. These are the ones who did not reach Colchis.

Moreover, on the voyage back, Eribotes, son of Teleon, and Canthus, son of ...cerion,[13] were killed in Libya by the shepherd Cephalion, brother of Nasamon, son of the nymph Tritonis and Amphithemis, whose flock they were pillaging with clubs. Also, Mopsus, son of Amphicus, died of a serpent's bite in Africa. He had joined the Argonauts during their voyage, after his father Ampycus had been murdered.

Likewise, the sons of Phrixus and Medea's sister Chalciope, Argus, Melas, Phrontides, and Cylindrus, joined them on the island of Dia. Others say they were called Phronius, Demoleon, Autolycus, and Phlogius.[14] When Hercules took them as companions, when he sought the girdle of the Amazons, he left them struck with terror. [Also joining was] Dascylus, son of the king of the Maryiandini.[15]

Moreover, when they had sailed forth for Colchis, they wanted to make Hercules their leader. He declined, saying that Jason, in whose service they were all sailing forth, should give the orders. Therefore, Jason ruled. Argus, son of Danaus, was builder. Tiphys was helmsman, after whose death Ancaeus, son of Neptune, guided the ship. Lynceus, son of Aphareus, who was able to see many things, was the lookout while sailing. The *toicharchoi*[16] were Zetes and Calaïs, sons of Aquilo, who had wings on their heads and feet. At the prow and oars sat Peleus

---

[13] The text is again corrupt here. The traditional father of Canthus is Cantheus.

[14] Several names were lost in the list, and the final three should be attributed as sons of Deimachus.

[15] The text is corrupt here, too. Dascylus acted as a guide for the Argonauts in Apollonius' *Argonautica* (2.802ff).

[16] Hyginus provides a Latin transliteration of the Greek for "superintendents of rowers."

and Telamon. At the center bench sat Hercules and Idas. The others kept their assigned seats. Orpheus, son of Oeagrus, gave the bosun's calls. Later, when Hercules had left, in his place sat Peleus, son of Aeacus.

This is the ship Argo, which Minerva carried up into the circle of stars because it had been built by her. The ship when first launched into the open sea appeared among the stars from rudder to sails. Cicero, in the *Phaenomena*,[17] described its beauty and appearance in the following verses:

> Creeping by the tail of the Dog,[18] the Argo glides
> Carrying her stern first, with its light[19]
> Not as other ships which place their prows first upon the deep,
> Cutting the meadows of Neptune with their bows
> But backward she carries herself through the spaces of the revolving sky
> As when sailors begin to reach safe harbors
> They turn the ship with its great burden
> And drag the stern backward to the welcome shore
> Thus ancient Argo glides backward over the heavens
> Thence her rudder, hanging from the soaring stern,
> Touches the back feet of the gleaming Dog.

This ship has four stars on her stern, on the right rudder five, on the left four, in total thirteen, themselves all very much alike.[20]

---

[17] This passage is originally from Aratus (*Phaenomena* 342ff.), whose *Phaenomena* was an epic poem of star lore. Cicero translated, expanded, and adapted Aratus' work into Latin hexameters (*Phaenomena aratea*), largely during his school years, which translation (371ff.) Hyginus uses. The poem refers to the former constellation of Argo Navis, which seems to travel backward across the night sky.

[18] I.e., the constellation Canis.

[19] I.e., a bright star.

[20] I.e., stars of the constellation Argo Navis are of similar magnitude.

15. Women of Lemnos

The women on the island of Lemnos for some years had not made a sacrifice to Venus, who in her anger made their men take Thracian wives and scorn their previous wives. But the Lemnian women, under the instigation of Venus, conspired to kill the whole clan of men there, except for Hypsipyle, who in secret placed her father Thoantes on a boat, which a storm carried to the island of Taurica. Meanwhile, the Argonauts, sailing along, came to Lemnos. When Iphinoe, the gatekeeper, saw them, she announced it to Queen Hypsipyle, to whom Polyxo, endowed with age, advised that she should bind them to the gods of hospitality and summon them to entertainment. Hypsipyle begot from Jason the sons Euneus and Deipylus. There they held back for many days; by Hercules' chiding, they departed. Moreover, after the Lemnian women learned that Hypsipyle had saved her father, they attempted to kill her. She fled. Pirates captured her, brought her to Thebes, and sold her in slavery to King Lycus. Also, the Lemnian women made pregnant by the Argonauts imposed their names[21] on their sons.

*   *   *

---

[21] I.e., the names of the Argonauts.

16. Cyzicus

Cyzicus, son of Eusorus, king of an island in the Propontis, received the Argonauts with generous hospitality. When they had left him and had sailed for a whole day, by a storm that arose by night they were brought unaware to the same island. Cyzicus, believing them to be Pelasgican enemies, brought arms against them by night on the shore, and was killed by Jason.[22] On the next day, when he[23] had come near the shore and saw that he had killed the king, he gave him burial and handed the kingdom to his[24] sons.

17. Amycus

Amycus, son of Neptune and Melie, was king of Bebyricae. All who came to his kingdom he compelled to contend with him in boxing, and he would destroy the losers. When in this place he challenged the Argonauts to boxing, Pollux contended with him and killed him.

18. Lycus

Lycus, king of an island in Propontis, received the Argonauts with hospitality and in honor because they had killed Amycus, who had often repudiated him. While the Argonauts were

---

[22] In the *Orphic Argonautica*, Heracles kills Cyzicus.

[23] Jason.

[24] The sons of Cyzicus.

staying with Lycus, and had gone out for straw,[25] Idmon died from being gored by a boar. Then, because he delayed a long time at the tomb, Tiphys, son of Phorbas, died. Then the Argonauts gave over control of the ship to Ancaeus, son of Neptune.

19. Phineus

Phineus, son of Agenor, a Thracian, had two sons by Cleopatra. They were blinded by their father due to their stepmother's accusations. Now, too, Apollo is said to have given this Phineus the power of prophecy. When he revealed the gods' plans, he was blinded by Jove, and he had set over him the Harpies, which are said to be the dogs of Jove, to carry away the food from his mouth. When the Argonauts came there and they asked him to show them the way, he said he would show them if they freed him from his punishment. Then Zetes and Calaïs, sons of the wind Aquilo and Orythia, who are said to have had wings on their heads and feet, chased away the Harpies to the Strophada Islands and freed Phineus from his punishment. He revealed how to cross the Symplegades: they should send out a dove; when the rocks had clashed together, on their retreat [they should row forth if the dove survived, but if the dove should die,][26] they should turn back. The Argonauts, through the kindness of Phineus, passed through the Symplegades.

*   *   *

---

[25] The same corruption occurs as in Fabula 14. Again, the meaning "left the walls" appears to be the more likely original reading.

[26] The text is again corrupt here and has been restored.

20. Stymphalides

When the Argonauts came to the island of Dia and the birds pierced them with arrows made from their feathers, when they were not able to withstand the great number of birds, by the advice of Phineus they took up their round shields and spears, and in the manner of the Curetes,[27] chased them away with noise.

21. Sons of Phrixus

When the Argonauts had gone through the Blue Rocks, which they call the Symplegades Rocks, into the sea which is called the Euxine and were wandering, by the will of Juno they were carried to the island of Dia. There they found shipwrecked, naked, and helpless the sons of Phrixus and Chalciope: Argus, Phrontides, Melas, and Cylindrus. When they explained their plight to Jason, that when they were hastening to go to their grandfather Athamas they had been shipwrecked and cast up there, Jason took them in and gave them help. They led Jason to Colchis by means of the river Thermodon, and now when they were not far from Colchis, they commanded him to place the ship in a hidden spot; and they went to their mother Chalciope, Medea's sister, and revealed the kindness of Jason and why he had come. Then Chalciope indicated about Medea and brought her to Jason with her[28] sons. When she saw him, she recognized the one whom she had fallen in love with in a dream

---

[27] I.e., the Korybantes, the armed dancers for Cybele, who banged on their shields to make a great noise.

[28] Chalciope's.

instigated by Juno, and she promised him everything; and they led him to the temple.

22. Aeëtes

Aeëtes, son of the Sun, was told that he would keep his kingdom so long as the Fleece, which Phrixus had dedicated, stayed in the sanctuary of Mars. And so Aeëtes gave Jason this task if he wished to take away the Golden Fleece: to yoke with an adamantine yoke the brazen-footed bulls who breathed flames from their nostrils, and plow, and sow from a helmet the teeth of the dragon from which would rise up a tribe of armed men who would kill one another. However, Juno wished to save Jason from this because when she had come to a river to test the minds of men, she pretended to be an old woman and asked them to carry her across; when others who crossed over expressed contempt for her, he[29] carried her across. And so, because she knew that Jason would not be able accomplish the commands without the help of Medea, she asked Venus to instill Medea with love. At Venus' incitement, Jason was loved by Medea; by her aid he was freed from all danger. For, when he had plowed with the bulls and the armed men sprang up, he threw a stone among them by Medea's counsel; they fought among themselves and killed one another. Moreover, when the dragon was put to sleep with drugs, he took the Fleece from the sanctuary and departed for his homeland with Medea.

* * *

---

[29] Jason.

23. Absyrtus

When Aeëtes had learned that Medea had escaped with Jason, he prepared a ship and sent his son Absyrtus in pursuit of her with armed companions. When he had overtaken her in the Adriatic Sea in Histria at the court of King Alcinous and wished to fight for her with arms, Alcinous intervened between them so they would not fight; they took him up as judge, and he postponed until the next day. When he seemed sad and he was asked by his wife Arete what was the cause of his sadness, he said that he had been made judge between two opposing communities, between the Colchians and the Argives. When Arete asked what judgment he would render, Alcinous responded, if Medea were a virgin, she would return to her father; but if a wife,[30] she would go to her husband. When Arete heard this from her husband, she sent a warning to Jason, and by night he deflowered Medea in a cave. Moreover, the next day when they came for the judgment and Medea was found to be a wife, she was handed over to her husband. Nevertheless, when they had departed, Absyrtus, fearing his father's orders, pursued them to the island of Minerva; in that place when Jason was sacrificing to Minerva and Absyrtus found him, he was killed by Jason. Medea gave burial to his body, and thence they departed. The Colchians who had come with Absyrtus, fearing Aeëtes, remained there, and they founded a town which from Absyrtus' name they called Absoros. Moreover, this island is located in Histria, opposite Pola, adjoining the island of Canta.[31]

---

[30] I.e., deflowered.

[31] This sentence is corrupt.

24. Jason and the Daughters of Pelias

Since Jason had undertaken so many trials by order of his uncle Pelias, he began to think how he could kill him without suspicion. This Medea promised to do. And so when they were now far from Colchis, she ordered the ship to be hidden in a secret place and she came herself to the daughters of Pelias as a priestess of Diana; she promised to make their father Pelias from an old man to a young man, but the oldest daughter, Alcestis, denied this was possible to do. Medea, who easily bent her to her will, threw mist before them and from drugs made many marvels, which looked to be like reality: She threw an old ram into a brazen cauldron, from which a very beautiful lamb seemed to spring forth. And so, in the same way, the daughters of Pelias, that is, Alcestis, Pelopia, Medusa, Pisidice, and Hippothoe, by the incitement of Medea, slew their father and boiled him in the brazen cauldron. When they saw that they had been deceived, they fled their homeland. But Jason, by a sign from Medea, seized the palace and handed to Acastus, son of Pelias and brother of the daughters of Pelias, his father's power, because he had gone with him to Colchis. He himself departed with Medea for Corinth.

25. Medea

When Medea, the daughter of Aeëtes and Idyia, had already begotten two sons from Jason, Mermerus and Pheres, and they were living in the greatest harmony, it was thrown in his teeth that a man so brave and handsome and noble should have for a wife a foreigner and a sorceress. Creon, son of Menoecus, king of Corinth, gave him his younger daughter Glauce as a wife. When Medea saw that she who had done good by Jason was afflicted with indignity, she made a golden crown from poison and she ordered her sons to give it to their stepmother as a gift. Accepting the gift, Creusa[32] burned to death with Jason and Creon.[33] When Medea saw the palace burning, she killed her children from Jason, Mermerus and Pheres, and fled from Corinth.

---

[32] A Roman name for Glauce, from the Greek for "princess."

[33] This version differs from the better-known story in Euripides' *Medea*.

The character of Dares Phrygius (Dares the Phrygian) first appears in Homer's *Iliad* as a wealthy priest of Hephaestus (5.9-10). In the second century CE, Claudius Aelianus (Aelian) mentions him as a writer of a poem on the Trojan War in his *Various History* (11.2): "They say also that *Dares* the *Phrygian*, whose *Phrygian* Iliad I know to be yet extant, was before *Homer*" (trans. Thomas Stanley).

The text that survives under Dares' name, the *Trojan History*, purports to be an eyewitness account of the Trojan War; however, the style and language of the text tell us that it could not have been written even as early as Aelian. Instead, it appears to be a fifth century CE work, roughly contemporary with the *Orphic Argonautica*, which pseudo-Dares would appear to mention if his words are taken literally (see note 2, p. 78).

In the Middle Ages, the *Trojan History* was ascribed to the first century BCE writer Cornelius Nepos, though it is almost certainly not his work; it is unknown whether the surviving text is an epitome of an older Latin work, an adaptation of a Greek work, or an original piece. Whatever its origins, the first three sections of Dares' account, translated here, would remain one of the few sources of information for Jason's adventures during the medieval period.

The Trojan History of Dares Phrygius
(Sections 1-3)

Pelias, king of the Peloponnese,[1] had a brother, Aeson. Aeson's son was Jason, of outstanding courage: and they who were within the kingdom, all of them he had as friends, and he was loved powerfully by them. King Pelias, when he saw that Jason had been accepted by all, feared that he would do him injury, or expel him from the kingdom. He told Jason that something worthy of his power lay in Colchis, the Golden Fleece of a ram; if he would snatch it away from there, Pelias promised to give over all power to him. When Jason heard this, since he was the bravest of souls, and wanted to know all things, and thought he would be more famous than anyone if he were to fetch the Golden Fleece, he told King Pelias he wanted to go if resources and associates were not lacking. King Pelias ordered the master-builder Argus summoned, and he ordered him to build the most beautiful boat he could, to Jason's every desire. The rumor galloped throughout all Greece that a ship was being built and that Jason was going to Colchis to ask for the Golden Fleece. Friends and strangers came to Jason and promised they would go. Jason gave his thanks to them, and he asked them to prepare for when the time would come. When the time had come, Jason sent letters to those who had promised to go, and they

---

[1] Pelias traditionally reigned in Thessaly. Later medieval writers confused him with Peleus, father of Achilles, so perhaps the writer here is confusing Pelias' kingdom of Iolcus in Thessaly with that of Peleus' ancestors in Aegina, an island near the Peloponnesus. The First Vatican Mythographer follows Darius (see p. 86).

immediately convened at the ship, whose name was Argo. King Pelias ordered that which was needed placed in the ship, and he urged Jason and those who were going with him to go with great courage to accomplish that which they were attempting. This event would bring glory to Greece and themselves. To describe those who set out with Jason is not our purpose: But he who wishes to know about them, let him read the *Argonautica*.[2]

Jason, when he had come to Phrygia, brought up the ship to the port of the Simoeis River. Then, they all disembarked from the ship for dry land. It was announced to Laomedon, King of the Trojans, that a ship had unexpectedly entered the port of the Simoeis River and young men had come in it from Greece. When Laomedon heard this he was disturbed, and he thought it a danger to the public if Greeks should be in the habit of landing on his shores in their ships. And so he sent word to the port for the Greeks to depart from his territory; and if they did not obey his word, then he would expel them from his territory by force. Jason and those who had come with him were deeply upset by the cruelty with which Laomedon was treating them; he had received no injury from them: and at the same time they were afraid to attempt to continue on against the order lest they be crushed by the multitude of barbarians. As they were not ready to do battle, they boarded the ship, retreated from the land, set out for Colchis, obtained the Fleece, and returned home.

---

[2] Since Dares claims to be writing at the time of the Trojan War, the actual writer either is referring to an otherwise unattested pre-Homeric *Argonautica* or has taken the *Orphic Argonautica* as the actual work of the Argonaut Orpheus before the Trojan War. Literary analysis of specific details used by Dares, however, indicates that Valerius Flaccus' poem is anachronistically the one meant by Dares.

Hercules was deeply upset at the insulting manner in which Laomedon had treated him and those who had set out for Colchis with Jason, and he came to Sparta, to Castor and Pollux.[3] He urged them to prosecute their injuries with him, lest Laomedon continue prohibiting others from his port and land with impunity. He said many others would follow if they devoted themselves to the cause. Castor and Pollux promised to do everything Hercules wanted.[4]

---

[3] Castor was the son of the Spartan king Tyndareus.

[4] Hereafter, Dares continues with an account of Hercules' raid on Troy, and then the history of the Trojan War proper.

Unfortunately, virtually nothing is know of the author or authors who passed under the name of Lactantius Placidus, the attribution of the writer of a series of summaries of Ovid's *Metamorphoses* composed sometime in late Antiquity. Often called the *Narrations* in early English, the more correct title, from the Latin, would be the *Summaries of the Stories of Ovid*. These summaries were drastic condensations of Ovid's text, with some additional material derived from sources including Hyginus and Statius. As a convenient abstract of the *Metamorphoses*, these summaries were included in some copies of Ovid, and in the Renaissance they served as a handbook of mythology for, among others, Boccaccio. As late as the eighteenth century, versions of these summaries appeared in published copies of Ovid. The texts given below are translated from the Latin edition prepared by Hugo Magnus in 1914.

The Narrationes of Lactantius
(Book 7: 1-4)

Fabula 1: The Teeth of a Dragon into Men

Jason, son of Aeson, was sent by Pelias, son of Neptune, with the nobles of Greece to Colchis to bring back the Golden Fleece, with Juno and Minerva as helpers so that he might reach the palace of Aeëtes, son of the Sun, and with his beauty turn Medea against her father, so that she would prefer to advise him rather than her father. Therefore she bound Jason into a promise of matrimony. She began to prepare Jason with drugs and spells for the fire-breathing bulls and the dragon guarding the temple and the Golden Fleece so that he could sew the teeth of the dragon, from which armed men would arise. Among them, he was taught by Medea, he must throw a stone so that they would fight among themselves and kill one another. This he managed, and Jason fled to Corinth with Medea.

Fabula 2: Aeson from Old Age to Youth

After carrying off Medea from her parents, Jason led her to Greece. With a promised marriage, he had sex with her. On account of the many fruits of her ingenious arts, he begged her to strike down his father Aeson's old age and lead him back to youth.

And she, not yet having put down her love for him that had seized her in youth, denied him nothing. She set up a bronze cauldron and cooked herbs of which she had knowledge, sought from various regions. She paid careful attention to a stake which was turning in the herbs. It changed into an olive tree laden with fruit, which, having been removed from the bronze cauldron, fell onto the ground. Thinking the time was right, killing Aeson, she mixed him with the moist herbs, and, as she had promised her husband, he was seen to be led from old age into pristine vigor.

Fabula 3: The Nurses of Liber into Youth

Having seen Medea expel Aeson's old age with her medicines, Father Liber asked her to help his nurses in the same way and lead them back to youthful vigor. Driven by his authority, by the medicines she had used on Aeson, she restored them to the first fruits of youth. She gave Liber an everlasting favor.

Fabula 4: A Ram Is Seen in the Appearance of a Lamb

After they saw a ram loaded down with years change form into a lamb, the Peliads, the daughters of Pelias, began ingratiatingly asking Medea to restore to their father Pelias the youth lost over the procession of time. She agreed, wanting to seize the opportunity to give punishment to the enemy of Jason. She impelled them to kill their father, and they dropped the cut up pieces of him into the boiling bronze cauldron. After this was done, Medea mounted a chariot drawn by dragons and, rising through the air, escaped from the sight of her enemies.[1]

---

[1] Hereafter, Lactantius summarizes Ovid's description of Medea's further adventures, noting that after much wandering on her "winged serpents" Medea came to Ephyra (the ancient name of Corinth), where, upon discovering Jason had remarried, by Medea's wrath Creon and Creusa were "set aflame by burning poison, the children abandoned by Jason done away with by her." Lactantius then summarizes Medea's adventures in Athens and beyond.

The three Vatican mythographers, otherwise anonymous, are so named because their three books of mythology were found bound together in the Vatican archive. The first of these documents, known as the text of the First Vatican Mythographer, is frequently suggested to have been written around the ninth or tenth century CE based upon the dating of the most recent sources the author used. The author is anonymous and writes in a plain, direct style with little additional commentary. I have made the translation of the four chapters devoted to the story of Jason and the Golden Fleece from the **1803** first edition and **1834** corrected printing of the Latin text of the Mythographer, including variant spellings and mistakes the Mythographer made in his storytelling. Note, for example, that the author confuses Pelias and Peleus, as well as the dragon whose teeth Jason sewed and the dragon Jason killed. Additional references to incidents touching on the Argonauts' journey occur in the work, but the following chapters are those that deal primarily with Jason.

The First Vatican Mythographer
(23-25, 188)

23. On Phrixus and Helle

Phrixus and Helle were siblings and the children of King Athamas and Nephele. When they were wandering in the woods they were stricken with madness by Liber. Their mother Nephele is said to have come to them and presented them with a ram distinguished by its golden fleece and ordered her children to climb up on the aforementioned ram and to go to King Oeeta[1] in Colchis and there sacrifice the ram. – Or, in another version: When Nephele, who is also Nubes, incited by the madness of Father Liber, made for the woods and did not return to her husband's hearth, Athamas brought home a stepmother named Ino for his children Phrixus and Helle: plotting death from a stepmother's hatred, she asked the matrons to destroy the grain that was to be sewn; for which reason a famine was born. When the community had sent to Apollo for a consultation, Ino bribed those who had been sent to report that the oracle said the children of Nephele must be sacrificed: and she said they had burned the grain. Their father, fearing the hatred of the people, entrusted the children to their stepmother's judgment, but in secret he gave them a remedy: For he sent forth Phrixus, ignorant of his own death, to lead away the ram that had the Golden Fleece. Urged on by the command of Juno to run away with

---

[1] I.e., Aeëtes.

his sister, he forthwith escaped death with her. Then when they floated above the sea while clinging to the ram, the girl Helle fell down into the sea: For from her it is called the Hellespont. Phrixus, delivered to Colchis, sacrificed the ram and consecrated the Golden Fleece in the temple of Mars, where an unsleeping dragon guarded it. King Oeeta received Phrixus cheerfully, and he gave him a daughter as a wife. When Phrixus received children from her, Oeeta, so that he would not expel him from the kingdom (for he had been given a divine prophesy to beware death by a foreigner), killed Phrixus. But his sons climbed into a ship to go over to their grandfather Athamas. Aeson received them after they were shipwrecked. Afterward, Jason set out for Colchis to take the Golden Fleece, and he killed the dragon, and he took away the Fleece.

24. On Pelias and Jason

Pelias, or Peleus,[2] king of the Peloponnesus, was the brother of Aeson, whose son was named Jason. Accordingly, the aforementioned Pelias feared his brother's son due to his strength and uprightness, lest he might expel him from the kingdom. And for this reason he sent him to Colchis, thence to bring back the Golden Fleece on which Jupiter had ascended to the heavens.[3] For he thought this would cause Jason's death. But a certain Argus made a ship which was called Argo after his name; and after this ship, Jason and his companions were called Argonauts. In truth, Typhis was the steersman. While sailing to

---

[2] The writer here confuses Aeson's brother with Achilles' father, a common problem in medieval retellings of Jason's story. For Peloponnesus, see p. 77 note 1.

[3] This is the first mention of the story of Jupiter's ascension, later repeated by other authors. It is perhaps a confused version of Jupiter (Zeus) placing the ram among the stars as the constellation Aries.

Colchis, en route they came to Troy: King Laomedon of Troy did not allow them to go into the port. Then they went back and told of what King Laomedon of Troy did to them. For this reason Pelias and Hercules came to Troy, by whom it was conquered and Laomedon killed.

25. On Jason

Under the command of Apollo's oracle, Jason sought to snatch the Golden Fleece, which Phrixus had consecrated to Mars. To get hold of it, he must first place under the yoke two bulls that were untamable among the Colchians. Medea, the greatest of sorceresses, marveled at his beauty. Through her sorcery, she drove him to bring the bulls under the yoke and to kill the sleepless dragon. He sewed its teeth once it was killed[4] and the bulls breathing Vulcan's fire yoked: the men born from this cut one another down with mutual wounds. Moreover, King Oeeta had proposed these conditions to him, for Apollo had answered that he would continue to reign so long as the Fleece was in the temple. After taking possession of the Golden Fleece, Jason later had Medea as a wife. But when he brought in a mistress of the name Glauce, daughter of Creon, Medea gave the mistress a tunic laced with poison and garlic: When she had put it on, she began to be burned alive by fire. Then Medea, not putting up with the soul of Jason raging against her, fled on a winged serpent.

*   *   *

---

[4] The writer conflates the dragon of Ares killed by Cadmus with the dragon of Colchis subdued by Jason. In later medieval works, this version became standard.

188. On Medea, Jason, Aeson, and the Nurses of Father Liber

After Jason had led Medea to Greece, he had sex with her, as he had promised her marriage. As she was a clever expert in many things, he asked her to restore his father Aeson's youth. As the love she had for him had not yet been put aside, refusing him nothing, she set up a bronze cauldron and cooked many kinds of plants which she knew and had obtained from diverse regions. She immersed Aeson, who had been killed, in the warm herbs, and she brought him through in his original vigor. When Father Liber noticed that Aeson's old age had been expelled by Medea's medicines, he asked her to bring help to his nurses and to restore them to the vigor of youth. Impelled by his authority and assistance, she gave to Liber an everlasting favor by the same medicines with which she had restored Aeson to his first blush of youth.

The Second Vatican Mythographer is believed to have written at an uncertain date sometime after the First Mythographer, perhaps during the Carolingian period. The anonymous author and copies much of the first Mythographer nearly word for word, with additional information added in from other sources. I have made the translation of five chapters devoted to the story of Jason and the Golden Fleece from the 1803 first edition and 1834 corrected printing of the Latin text of the Mythographer, including the variant spellings and non-traditional versions of the myths the writer incorporated. As with the First Mythographer, additional references to incidents touching on the Argonauts' journey occur in the work, but the following chapters are those that deal primarily with Jason. The Third Vatican Mythographer chose not to tell the Argonauts' story directly.

The Second Vatican Mythographer
(134-138)

134. On King Athamas

King Athamas, son of Aeolus and brother of Creteius, had a wife called Nubes or Nephele, from whom he received Phrixus and Helle. When therefore Nubes, stirred up by the madness of Father Liber, had made for the woods and did not want to return to her husband's hearth, Athamas put over his children a stepmother named Ino, who, with a stepmother's hatred and plotting the death of the children, asked the matrons to destroy the grain to be sown. Because of this deed, a famine arose. Moreover, when the community sent to Apollo for a consultation, Ino bribed him who had been sent to report that the oracle said Nubes' children were to be sacrificed. For and in fact she had said they had set the grain on fire. In truth, their father, fearing the hatred of the people, handed over his children to the judgment of their stepmother: When their hostile stepmother was pursuing them as they were wandering in the woods, it is said their mother came to them and presented to them a ram distinguished by Golden Fleece. Under the compulsion of Juno, she ordered the aforementioned children to climb up on the ram and to go over to the island of Colchis, to King Oeta, son of the Sun, and there to sacrifice the aforementioned ram. Obeying their mother's command, the ram carried them over the sea. Helle, as a girl of the weaker sex, slipped off and gave her name to the Hellespont. Phrixus arrived at Colchis, and there, obeying his mother's order, he sacrificed the ram and consecrated its Golden Fleece in the temple of Mars, where it is said he placed an always watchful dragon as guardian.

135. On Pelias

An oracular response was given to Pelias, son of Neptune, who possessed the summit of Iolcus, that he would be deprived of his citadel by one who would arrive there with one bare foot at the same time as he was making a sacrifice to Neptune. Therefore, when Pelias was making the annual sacrifice to his father Neptune, Jason, the son of Aeson, having lost one sandal in the mud of the River Anaurus, came to him wearing a sandal on only one foot. Pelias observed him, and remembering the oracles, he sent him forth under the appearance of glory, yet with the intention that a dragon would kill him on account of him seeking the Golden Fleece from King Oeta in Colchis. But an oracle had been made to Oeta that he would be able to remain in his kingdom only so long as the Golden Fleece remained in the temple of Mars. Eager to acquire the Golden Fleece, Jason assembled the courageous men of Greece: He received Hercules and Castor with his brother.[1] And after a ship called Argo was built, whence they were called Argonauts, Tiphis was made helmsman, and Jason set out to enter a formerly untried sea.

*   *   *

---

[1] Pollux.

136. On Jason

Moreover, when the ship Argo was built on Mount Pelius[2] in Thessaly, the earth, grieving that the previously untouched sea had become traversable, hurled rocks into the sea. Because those who were building the ship saw this, they sent her unfinished into the sea. Thus Lucan: "Carried away with smaller stern, the Argo is hauled down the mountain"[3]: for indeed the whole ship is not formed in the sky but only from the helm to the mast.[4] Moreover, when they had come to Colchis, Jason, welcomed by King Oeta, fell in love with the king's daughter Medea and had sons by her. But Oeta, after receiving an answer from oracles to beware of death from a stranger from the family of Aeolus, killed Phrixus, whose sons boarded a boat to cross over to their grandfather Athamas.[5] They were received by Aeson after being shipwrecked. Moreover, Jason, although eager to remove the Golden Fleece, feared the ever-watchful dragon he saw. King Oeta conceded him the opportunity to carry off the Fleece under this condition: if he would yoke bulls that breathed fire from their nostrils and were untamable by the Colchians and then sow the teeth of the dragon. Although this seemed difficult to him, Medea, the magical daughter of King Oeta, taking pleasure in his strength, loved him. Medea cast a spell over the serpent and put it to sleep; at once Jason killed it and took its teeth. After he had yoked the bulls breathing fire from their nostrils by Medea's wiles, he crossed into the field and sowed.

---

[2] Pelion.
[3] *Pharsalia* 2.717.
[4] As the constellation Argo Navis.
[5] The son of Aeolus.

On the third day an armed army rose up from that place and made an attack on Jason. Then by Medea's arts they were inflamed against themselves and killed each other with mutual wounds. Jason, receiving victory, seized the Fleece and took it away. Then Medea, abandoning Colchis and following Jason, is said to have reached Italy, and she taught remedies against snakes to the people living around Lake Fucinum; and also by these people she was called Anguitia because the snakes were vexed[6] by her magical formulae.

137. On Medea

After Jason led Medea to Greece, he had sex with her as he had promised her marriage. Having seen her clever skills in many things before, eventually he asked her to transform his father Aeson into young manhood. She had not yet put aside the love she had for him. Boiling in a bronze cauldron plants whose power she knew, obtained from diverse regions, she cooked the slain Aeson with warm herbs and restored him to his original vigor.

138. On the Nurses of Liber

When Father Liber noticed that Aeson's old age had been expelled by Medea's medicines, he entreated Medea to change his nurses back to the vigor of youth. Agreeing to his request, she established a pledge of eternal benefit with him by restoring his nurses to the vigor of youth by giving them the same medicines that had rejuvenated Aeson. But when Jason, spurning her, took in

---

[6] Latin: *angere*, "torment," but also likely punning on *anguis*, "snake."

Glauce, the daughter of Creon, Medea gave his mistress a tunic laced with poison and garlic: When she put it on, she began to burn alive by fire. Then Medea, not putting up with the soul of Jason raging against her, did away with her and Jason's sons and fled on a winged serpent.

Appendixes

Appendix A
Translation of Part of the *Argonautics of Orpheus*[1]

William Preston

The account of *Orpheus,* or whoever was the ancient poet, whether *Onomacritus,*[2] or any other, who composed the account of the *Argonautic* expedition, which has reached us, and is certainly of very remote antiquity, and borrowed in great measure from the *Orphic* fables and traditions, differs, in many circumstances, from the narrative of *Apollonius;* and particularly with respect to the route, which the adventurers pursued, on their return from *Colchis* to *Greece.*—The reader will not be displeased to see this account, as it is given by the venerable author.

Arg. v. 1020.—*Æetes* suddenly heard from his servants, that *Medea* was borne away, and presently ordered *Absyrtus* to assemble the people, and go in quest of his sister. The youth, without loss of time, hastened to the banks of the river, to the vessel of the heroes; and there he found the unhappy virgin. Night, meantime, adorned with stars, had performed half her course, when the horrid fraud, the black and portentous deed of *Medea,* was perpetrated on *Absyrtus,* at the suggestion of love.—For she, and her accomplices, killing him, cast the pieces of his mangled body towards the banks, of the rapid river, which, being agitated by a powerful wind, hurried him away. The remains of the unhappy youth, were borne to the sea, and cast, at length, length, upon certain islands, which still retain the name of *Absyrtus.*—This cruel deed did not pass unnoticed, by all-seeing *Jove* and *Nemesis.*

After the *Argonauts* had embarked on board their vessel, and cut the halsers on each side, from the banks of the river, and bending more and more on their swift oars, cut the river; we were not borne strait forward, to the fishy sea, through the mouth of the broad *Phasis,* but were borne about afar, by a wide deviation, perpetually sailing back. The cities of

---

[1] William Preston, *The Argonautics of Apollonius Rhodius,* vol. III (Dublin: 1803), 21-34.

[2] See Appendix B—J.C.

the *Colchians* were left behind, without the knowledge of the *Minyæ;* for a black and overshadowing night was diffused around. Thus labouring and astray, not knowing whither we went, we ran through the mid channel of the stream.—The people, who dwell around, are, the *Gymni,* the *Buonomæ,* the tribe of the *Corcetici,* and the clownish *Areyes,* with the ferocious *Sindi*—Here the *Argonauts* thought to pass among the habitations of the *Charandai,* near the ridges of *Caucasus,* through the narrow pass of *Erythia*. But, when morn appeared, delighting man, with her beams, we touched at a grassy island, surrounded by two rivers, whose streams are not navigable, the expansive *Phasis,* and the smoothly flowing *Sarangis*. The lake *Mæotis* inundating the land, sends the latter, through the reedy grass and sedge, resounding to the sea. Then, plying our oars, we sailed day and night—by two outlets of the lake we arrive at the *Bosporus*[3]—through the midst of this, *Titan,* mounted on a mighty bull, past, with the oxen which he had stolen, dividing the passage from the lake.[4]—Here, worn-out with the fatigue of rowing, through the weary length of day, we first arrive at the seats of the *Mæotæ,* softly robed—the race of the *Geloni*—the countless tribes of the long-haired *Comatæ,* the *Sauromatæ,* the *Getæ,* the *Gymnæi,* the *Cecryphæ*.—The ferocious and dangerous races of people, who dwell in the land around the lake *Mæotis*.—Yet still the gods set before us mighty toil and anguish—after we past, in the region of these people, the last waters of this abyss. There the water is confined with narrow banks, and inundates that savage and inhospitable land, with mighty noise—it swells, and the adjacent wood, trackless and vast, rebellows to the sound. At length, it disembogues itself in the ocean, and the boundaries of the north.— Thither the vessel past, hurried through the narrow strait. Through nine incessant nights and days our toil we ply. On either hand, we leave behind us uncounted tribes of savage men. The *Pacti,* the *Arctii,* the cruel *Lelii,* the *Scythians,* quivered all, the trusty servants of *Mars*. The *Tauri,* homicide race, who perform direful sacrifice to *Artemis,* and fill the consecrated chalice with human gore. We leave behind the *Hyperborei,* the *Nomades,* and the *Caspian* race. But when the tenth morn, enlightener of mortal man, appeared; we touched on the hollow vales

---

[3] The *Cimmerian Bosporus*.

[4] The *Palus Mæotis,* now called the sea of *Zabach*.

between the *Riphean* hills. There, on the instant, *Argo* rushed forth, dancing and bounding over the stream, and sprang into the ocean.— The *Chronian* sea, called by men the *Hyperborean* deep, or the *Dead Sea.*—There vanished all our hopes of escaping the most dreadful doom; and too fully had our fears been realised; but *Ancæus,* relying on the polished rudder, guided the ship, that rushed with mighty force, impelled, and compelled her to seek the right-hand shore. Forward she leaped, constrained by the great exertions of the rowers. When now our arms were fatigued, by long and painful efforts at the oars, and our hands could no longer grasp them. With sinking hearts we rested on our elbows, and supported our heavy heads that dropt with briny dew.— The pangs of hunger aggravated the sufferings of weariness. But *Ancæus* sprang forward, and roused and animated all the other heroes with his exhortations, addressing them in soothing terms.—Then, because of the tenacious mud, the heroes descended with well-twisted ropes, over the sides of the ship, let themselves down lightly into the sea, and two of them, *Ancæus* and *Argus,* supported us. They by ropes made fast an halser from the poop, and gave the ends of it to the grasp of the other heroes. They instantly hurried along the beach, hauled the rope with all their might, and the ship, formed to pass the seas, followed where they drew, cutting her liquid path through the waves, over the smooth pebbles of the beach.—No longer did the howling air, with blasts of roaring wind, excite the loud sea—in silence I left the deep, where the last wave of *Tethys,* and the northern bear, lies spread. When the sixth morn arose, enlightener of man, we came, with short interval, to a race rejoicing in wealth and affluence, the *Macrobians* they are called—they live for many years—twelve chiliads of months of a hundred years of the full moon, without any of the troublesome concomitants of age. But, when at last they have reached the month, appointed by fate, they sink in a sweet and tranquil slumber, and find the boundaries of life. Nor thoughts of food, nor other cares and toils, that molest the generality of men, breed in them the least solicitude. On sweet and fragrant herbs they feed, amid the verdant and grassy pastures, and drink ambrosial dew, divine potation. All resplendent alike, in coeval youth, a placid serenity for ever smiles on their brows, and lightens in their eyes, the consequence of a just temperament of mind and disposition, both in parents and in sons, perpetually disposing them to act what is just, and speak what is prudent. Through the populous region of these we past by land, and reached another shore—then, still dragging along our light-sailing vessel, we arrived at the region of the *Cimmerians,* who alone are unconscious of the splendour of the sun, that glows with flame; for the *Riphean* mountain, and the ridge of *Calpis,* intercept from them the radiance of the orient dawn, and enormous *Phlegra* projecting, darkens the noontide air, and the peaked *Alps* extended, a ridge immense, conceal from these people the departing rays of the evening sun; and darkness for ever broods over the region inhabited by them.—Thence departing, with unwearied feet, we arrived at a bluff and pointed promontory, and a harbour defended from the winds—there *Acheron,* whose currents wash down gold, laves a gelid region, and pours along his waters, clear and bright as silver—with blackening expanse, a deep and gloomy lake receives him. Along the banks of the river resound the murmur of whispering and luxuriant trees,that night and day are loaded with perennial fruit.—All around, *Ceres,* protectress of the fruitful earth, abundant source of food to roan, fills the stately walls, and well-built streets, with plenteousness—within those mansions abide a race of men, of transcendent integrity and justice. One bark suffices to waft them, when life is past—for instantly the parted shades are transferred, from that pleasant arm of the sea, to *Acheron.* For near them are set the dwelling and eternal gates of *Hades;* and near them the shadowy tribes, the realm of phantoms.

This city too we past, and these tribes of people; still pressing forward, to fulfil our woful and calamitous destiny. Then *Ancæus* advanced from the ship, and instantly directed all his companions, weary as they were, to embark in a throng. And thus he adrest them, in mild and soothing words.

"Endure, my friends, this labour also; for after this I trust, ye will not encounter any more severe. I feel the eastern wind blow strong, and curl the surface of the deep.—I find an indication of the rising wind, in the roaring of the waves over the sand; they never roar in vain. Quickly, then, upraise the mast, unfurl your sails, expand them from the shrouds, and trim your vessel for the voyage."

The crew exerted themselves to execute his orders. Then sudden, from the hollow womb of the vessel, was heard a tremendous voice. In thundering human tone the prophetic beech resounded, which *Pallas* had included within the timbers of the ship.—Thus it spoke, and consternation came on the spirits of all.—"Oh, wretched I!—better had I perished in the *Euxine* waves, dashed to pieces, and scattered on the surface of the deep, by the *Cyanean* rocks.—I should not, degraded and obscure, have borne Reproach and shame, through the ignorance of kings.—For now the fury, vengeful of kindred blood, follows in the rear, claiming her debt of punishment for slain *Absyrtus*—disaster on disaster presses down your heads.—Soon as I more nearly approach the vengeful sisters, I shall openly accuse you of the recent and deadly crime—unless turning me, with my consecrated head and stern, you guide me within the embayed recesses, where land surrounds the unproductive sea. That I may pass out over the *Atlantic* waves."

Thus having spoken, the sacred wood was mute. The souls of the *Minyæ* stood appalled.—They saw, that a direful fate impended, through the disastrous passion of *Jason*. And much they revolved, within their secret thoughts, whether it would not be expedient to kill the ill-fated *Medea,* their unlucky companion, and thus avert the wrathful pursuit of the furies. This purpose they had executed; and thrown her overboard, to feed the fishes of the deep; but touched with compassion, the renowned son of *Æson* observed them instantly, and frustrated their design; and with supplications interposed, to prevent its completion; and with entreaties appeased the mind of each of his companions.

After they had thus heard the prophetic voice of *Argo;* the heroes, without delay, sate down on the benches of rowers, and grasped their oars; and *Ancæus,* with skill, managed the helm. They past the island of *Hibernia,* in their course.—With impetuous vibration and attendant darkness, the wind arose in their wake and filled their swelling sails—the ship ran swiftly over the heaving billows—then not one of the heroes hoped any longer to escape destruction. For now the twelfth morn arose; and none of the crew could imagine or divine, within his mind, where we were. *Lynceus,* at length, discovered the bounds of the calmly flowing and tranquil ocean; for he descried, in the remote horizon, a certain island clad with pines, where are the spacious mansions of *Ceres,* queen among the gods. Around, it was enveloped, in thick clouds, and walls of mist.—Concerning the story of all these, O intelligent *Musæus,* you have already heard my historic song—how her kinsmen deceived *Persephone,* cropping the tender blossoms through the vast extended mead; and afterwards, how *Pluto* having yoked to the car his sable steeds, assailed the virgin with the permission of *Jupiter,* and bore her away by force, through the unproductive waves. Then, I refused to sail to the shore, and splendid mansions of that isle, where, never mortal had touched as yet, with adventurous prow. For it possesses not any harbour, which might receive the manageable ship. But a steepy rock, scaling Heaven, defends on every side the sea-girt coast: within whose cincture spring the grateful gifts of bounteous *Ceres.—Ancæus* then, the ruler of the ship with sable prow, was not unmindful of my caution, but quickly urging back the ship, he made her to recede, by inclining the rudder to the left hand then, that the vessel might not rush onward, he turned the rudder towards the right.

On the third day, we arrived at the residence of *Circe,* at the *Lycæan* land, stations surrounded by the sea. With anxious and sorrowful heart we touched on that shore. We bound our cables to the rocks, and *Jason* sent forward from the ship some of his chosen companions, with directions to proceed, and search what race of men inhabited that extensive region, and procure a knowledge of the habitations and manners of the people. Presently, the maid, the full sister of the magnanimous *Ætes, Circe,* daughter of the sun, met them, as they advanced—(*Circe*—so *Asterope* her mother, and the glorious *Hyperion* her father, call the nymph)—to the ship her course she bent—amazement seised the heroes, at the view—the tresses, waving from her head, were like beams of light—bright shone her beauteous countenance a subtle flame was dartd from her eyes—soon as she beheld *Medea,* through the disguise of her snowy veil (for opprest with shame and anguish, while pallid grief preyed on her heart, the maid had cast the floating drapery over her charms.)—Her *Circe* marked, and, moved with pity, addrest her in these terms.—

"Ah wretch, what fate has the *Cyprian* queen on thee imposed!—Think not, that the recent transactions, before your arrival at this, my isle, are hid from my view—hither you come, polluted by a twofold crime—rebellion against the legitimate authority of a father—and parricidal murder, stained as ye are with the blood of a brother, butchered in the most cruel manner.—Nor shall you, if aright I deem, arrive at your native lands—if, with fatal security, you persevere in your present career of guilt unexpiated, and neglect to cleanse and purify yourselves by rites of lustration.—No—hope not for prosperous return until you shall have averted the wrath of the deities, by religious rites, and sacrifices of atonement, at the shores of *Malæa,* under the direction of *Orpheus.*— But, think not, you, in your present plight, thus impious and unattoned, to pass my threshold. The gods forbid—stained and polluted as you are. Nevertheless, I shall send you, with prompt liberality, the gifts that hospitality requires—bread, and racy wine, and abundant viands, more than your wants demand."

Thus, having spoke, she returned with wings of speed—and forthwith, in the midst of the ship, abundance of vessels were set, prepared for food and potation; and every requisite for a banquet was disposed in order.—As we prepared for our departure, a vehement wind arose— resounding shrill, it breathed to waft the heroes on their course.—Then, loosing our cables from that island, we pass over the waves—we reach the strait of *Tartessus,* and touch at the pillars of *Hercules*—we delay, during the evening, at the promontory, sacred to potent *Bacchus;* compelled by the necessity of procuring sustenance.—When morn, the harbinger of light, awoke from regions of the east, we, with her dawn, awoke to our toils, and ploughed the green surface of the salt pro-found. —We arrived at the *Sardinian* sea—the gulfs of the *Latins*—*Ausonian* islands and *Tyrrhenian* shores—but after we had arrived at *Lilybæum,* and the surrounding channel, we touch on *Sicily,* a tri-angular island. There the *Ætnæan* flame of *Enceladus* retarded our progress, eager as we were. Then, suddenly over the prow the dreadful waves boiled up, from the secret bottom of the abyss, with mighty noise, and reached even our highest sails.—And there the devouring whirlpool detained the ship—nor suffered it to spring forward—or, on the other hand, to glide backward. But in the hollow of that fatal vortex she was whirled round and round. And now the *Argo* was in such a state, that she must quickly have been swallowed up in the deep devouring surge, had not *Eurybia,* eldest daughter of the hoary father of the deep, desired to behold her husband *Peleus,* gently emerging from the sea. She snatched from destruction the vessel of the *Argonauts,* and saved it from being sunk beneath the billows.

Then, pursuing our course not far from thence, we discovered a lofty and projecting rock, and over it hangs a steep and craggy cliff, eaten into vast caverns, within which the blackening waves rebellow dreadful.—Seated there, the nymphs deceitful utter sweet and insidious sounds, and sooth the hearing of mortals, who are destined never to return.—Then, were the *Minyæ* delighted, to listen to the blandishing song of the *Sirens*. And never had they sailed past that voice of pernicious sweetness.—And even now they were dropping the oars from their hands—and *Ancæus* had steered the ship directly towards the fatal promontory: had not I, taking the lyre in my hands, tried the chords, and sung the strain my mother taught, delightful ornament of minstrelsy;—I sung, and boldly smote the strings, in unison with the song.—The song was this—"How, formerly, the deities contended, concerning the steeds with feet of storm; and the dark-haired *Neptune,* enraged with, father *Jove,* struck, with his golden trident, the *Lyctenian* lands, and dissipated them over the vast expanse of sea, where they became isles, surrounded by the deep, which men denominated *Sardinia, Eubœa,* and the stormy *Cyprus.*"—Thus, as I struck the lyre, the *Sirens,* from the snowy summit of the rock, astonished heard. And their own song was intermitted.—One cast the flute, and one the vocal shell, from her hands; and dreadfully they groaned, for the fatal period of their destined annihilation was at hand Then, from the summit of the caverned and gaping rock, they precipitated themselves into the abysses of the sea, for ever toiling through its troubled billows.—There they changed into rocks their graceful forms, and transcendent charms.

When *Argo,* flying swiftly over the deep, had escaped also this mortal danger—while the winds filled her sails, and the shrouds were strained on the mast, she was wafted over the billows, and through the bays, and arrived at the divine *Corcyra*—there abode the *Pheacians,* skilled in navigation. *Alcinous,* the most just of kings, reigned over this people, and gave them laws and administered justice.—We furled our sails—we made fast our cables—we moored our ship, and prepared sacrifices to *Panomphæan Jove,* and *Epactian Apollo.*—Here, with mighty force, and an infinite number of vessels, the fleet of *Æetes* sailed up to us—with strenuous efforts they rowed along—the *Colchians,* the *Erravians,* the *Charandæans,* and the *Solymæans,* in pursuit of the *Minyæ,* that they might bring back *Medea* to the presence of her father, and make her responsible in punishment, for the crime of having murdered her brother. But when they approached more nearly the secret recess of the deep and capacious harbour—then their heralds proceeded without delay to the palace of *Æetes*.⁵—The knees of *Medea* were unnerved; and on her cheeks fear diffused its pallid hue—through apprehension, lest the *Pheacian* monarch should seise, and tend her, reluctant, to the residence of her father, and direful catastrophe should ensue.—But vindictive *Juno* conceded not the death of *Medea*—before that *Jason*, with her co-operation, had inflicted fell calamities on the house of *Pelias*, and on that king himself.—When they heard the purposes of the cruel *Colchian* king, even the beautiful *Aretè*, and the god-like *Alcinous*—*Alcinous* directed the heralds to take the maid, the subject of contention, from the tall ship, and bear her to her father, that she might suffer the punishment due to her guilt. But *Aretè*, the illustrious queen, pitied her, and with soft intercession addrest her husband. And spoke to this effect.

"A reprobated task it were, my husband, to rend the nuptial bond—to scatter to the winds the sacred marriage bed, and extinguish the hallowed torch of love—great is the wrath of *Dionæan Venus*, both at men and women, who meditate such deeds.—But, if *Medea* be yet a virgin, and has reached our shores untouched; let her depart to her father's home, and the tribes of the *Colchians*: but if she has exchanged her virgin flower, for intercourse with man, and conjugal embrace, let her spouse conduct her with him."

She spake; and her words sunk deep in the soul of *Alcinous*. And he determined to perform every thing as she advised.—Nor was the determination hid from the *Minyæ*—for *Juno*, without delay, having assumed the form of a slave, hasted to the ship, and succinctly, in hurried tone, related what the king desired.—Then, *Medea* prepared her nuptial couch, in the stern of the vessel; while others strewed the carpets, and extended around the golden fleece. They likewise hung the hides of bulls, and their shields and armour, all around, on spears, to conceal the mystic rites of the genial bed.—Thus were the ill-omened nuptials, of the hapless *Medea*, consummated.

When the *Colchians*, and the *Minyæ*, came to the presence of the blameless king, and respectively stated their pretensions and demands, the son of *Æson* obtained from *Alcinous* an award, that he should keep *Medea* as his wife. This having heard, the heroes quickly loosed the cables of the ship, and, by force of rowing, *Argo*, endowed with human

---

⁵ Preston here means Alcinous, not Aeëtes—J.C.

speech, fled quickly over the deep, and ploughed her way through the gulf of *Ambracia*.

Now, O *Musæus*, offspring of a goddess, I will relate to you all that the *Minyæ* endured after this, from stormy blasts, on the shores of the *Syrtis;* and how, at length, they were rescued from their course of weary wandering over the deeps; and what adversities they endured in *Crete;* when, wafted to that shore, they beheld the form terrific of the brazen giant, who prohibited all entrance within the harbour: and how, constrained by the roaring billows, and the sudden force of blackening tempests, we expected that our swift ship should be dashed on the gloomy and formidable rocks. But the far-shooting *Pæan* was near, propitious to our call—he heard us—he sent a shaft from craggy *Delos*—he revealed himself from the midst of the *Sporades.*— Hence, that island has been called *Cranae,* by all the men, who inhabit the circumjacent regions.— But it was not allowed wholly to prohibit the son of *Æson,* from navigating the deep, for he bore with him the price of his ransom.—Pernicious fate recoiled from her attempt; for grievous was the wrath of *Hyperion.*—Soon as by force of rowing the *Minyæ* gained the promontory of *Malta*—then, by the suggestions of *Circè,* they proceeded to deliver themselves from the curses *of Æetes,* and the persecuting fury exacting punishment for sin.—Then, I performed, on behalf of the *Minyæ,* the rites that expiate sin, and supplicated *Neptune,* whose trident shakes the earth, that he might grant a safe return, and the sight of our beloved native home, to the toil-worn train, and bless them in the embraces of their fond parents.

Again the *Argonauts* set their sail, and directed their course to the well-built *Iolcos.*—But I returned to the shady *Tenarus,* that I might perform sacrifices to the great and awful rulers, who preside over the shades, and hold the keys of the infernal prison house. Passing from thence, I directed my rapid course to snowy *Thrace, to* the region of *Libethrians,* my native land—and entered the far-famed cave, where the muse my mother bore me to the divine *Æagrus*.

Appendix B

The Age of the Argonautica of Orpheus[1]

E. H. Bunbury

I should have been content to leave the consideration of the supposed antiquity of the Argonautica, as was done by K. O. Müller and Mr. Grote, as a question that had been decided beyond appeal by the successive investigations of Schneider, Hermann, and Ukert: had it not been for its having been brought forward afresh by M. Vivien de St. Martin in his recent work on the historical progress of Geography.[2] Admitting that the arguments of the German critics, derived from grammatical and metrical details, may be conclusive against assigning an early date to the poem in its present shape, he still maintains that it may be merely a *rifacciamento* of an earlier work, and that the poem now extant is in substance the same as that of which he ascribes the composition to Onomacritus. Two arguments appear to me conclusive against this hypothesis: the one, that, as stated in the text, this supposed *redaction* by Onomacritus of a poem on the Argonautic voyage is a pure fiction: that is to say, a mere arbitrary hypothesis, assumed without a particle of evidence. There is *some* ancient authority, though very vague and indefinite, for Onomacritus having composed hymns in the name of Orpheus, or worked up previously existing poems of a religious character into a more definite shape; and it is not improbable that the poems current under the name of Orpheus in the time of Aristophanes belonged to this class. But there is absolutely *none* for Onomacritus having handled the subject of the Argonautics, a poem of a totally different character.[3] Nor, in the second place, is there any mention of the

---

[1] E. H. Bunbury, *A History of Ancient Geography among the Greeks and Romans from the Earliest Ages to the Fall of the Roman Empire*, vol. 1 (London: John Murray, 1879).

[2] *Histoire de la Géographie et des Déscouveretes Géographique*. 8 vo. Paris, 1875.

[3] Suidas, indeed, mentions a certain Orpheus *of Crotona* as having written a poem, called Argonautica (s. v.) And this Orpheus is evidently the same who is mentioned by another grammarian as having been associated with Onomacritus in the task of revising the poems of Homer. (Schol. ad Plaut. cited by Ritschl *Die Alexandrinische Bibliothek*,

existence of any such poem before the Alexandrian period, or indeed till long after; and the existing Scholia on Apollonius, which are of unusual fulness and value, while repeatedly referring to the different versions of the tale found in different authors, never allude to the existence of a poem on the subject under the imposing name of Orpheus. This consideration alone appears to me conclusive against its being of older date than the late Alexandrian period.

The internal evidence appears to me equally decisive. M. de St. Martin finds in it the primitive simplicity and didactic character of the earliest poets. To me it appears, in common with several distinguished critics, to have the jejune and prosaic tameness so characteristic of the declining Greek poetry of the second and third century after the Christian era. And this character is as strongly marked in the conception and mode of treatment of the subject as in the details of style and diction. For these last I must refer my readers to Hermann's elaborate dissertation, appended to his edition of the Orphica; an excellent summary of the whole subject, from the critical point of view, is given by Bernhardy in his *Grundriss der Griechischen Literatur* (2nd edition, Halle, 1856, vol. ii pp. 347-353).

From the geographical point of view it matters little whether the poem is to be ascribed to the Alexandrian or to the Christian period. In either case it is equally worthless, and unworthy of careful examination. But the evidence that it is not (as M. de St. Martin maintains) "certainly anterior to Herodotus," appears to me overwhelming. The confusion of the writer's geography, which is regarded by M. de St. Martin as arising from his great antiquity, bears a striking resemblance to that found in several of the later geographers. It is not merely that he has erroneous ideas, even in regard to regions like the north coasts of the Aegean; that he represents the Araxes, Thermodon, Phasis, and Tanais, as all having a common origin; and that in describing the voyage from the Maeotis to the Northern Ocean, he jumbles together the names of Scythian tribes derived from all kinds of sources, and enumerates the Geloni, Sauromatae, Getae, and Arimaspians, among the nations dwelling around the

---

p. 4.) He therefore nourished in the time of the Pisistratids. It is singular that more use has not been made of this statement of Suidas (*valeat quantum*), by the advocates of the early date of the poem.

Palus Maeotis, while he transfers the Tauri, noted for their human sacrifices, to the shores of the channel leading into the Northern Ocean. But he describes the Argonauts as passing through a narrow channel into the Ocean, "which is called by the Hyperborean tribes the Cronian Sea and the Dead Sea." Both these names were familiar to the geographers and poets of later, times; but no trace of them is found before the Alexandrian period. Here they visit in succession the Macrobians, Cimmerians, and the land of Hermionia, where is the mouth of Acheron and the descent into the infernal regions: but they are especially warned to avoid the island of Ierne, in order to do which they by great exertions double the Sacred Cape, and after twelve days' voyage reach the fir-clad island, sacred to Demeter, where the poet places the fable of the Rape of Persephone. Thence in three days they come to the island of Circe, after which they pass by the Columns of Hercules into the Sardinian Sea. Here we find mentioned the customary legends of the Sirens, Charybdis, &c, but mixed up with the names of the Latins, Ausonians, and Tyrrhenians, as inhabitants of its shores: and the mention of Lilybaeum in Sicily is associated with the burning Aetna, and the fable of Enceladus. It is remarkable that the "far-stretching Alps" are mentioned among the ranges of mountains—associated with the Rhipæan mountains and the Calpian ridge—that overshadowed the land of the Cimmerians, and helped to shut out from it the light of the sun. Absurd as is this statement, it shows a familiarity with the name of the Alps as a great mountain chain, though it was certainly unknown as such to the Greeks in the days of Herodotus. The mention of Ierne (or, as it is called in one passage, the Iernian Islands) is still more decisive. There is no evidence of any knowledge of the British Islands among the Greeks before the time of Pytheas, while the name of Ierne (Ireland) is not mentioned till a considerably later period.

Confused and extravagant as are the geographical notions contained in the above narrative, it does not appear to me possible to pronounce upon their evidence alone, that the poem cannot belong to the Alexandrian period instead of the Roman Empire. Its assignment to the later age must rest upon considerations of style and language, as well as upon the all-important fact that no allusion to its existence is found in any ancient author, or even in any of the scholiasts or grammarians down to a very late date.

Appendix C
On Valerius Flaccus and the *Orphic Argonautica*[1]

Walter Coventry Summers

There is, however, a Greek poem, written probably before 400 A.D. on the same subject as that of our author, and I am inclined to believe that we can find some traces of his poem here. I refer of course to the so-called Orphic Argonautica, the relation of which to the Latin work has not so far as I know been previously examined. The resemblances are (*a*) partly in the matter, and (*b*) partly in the language. As regards class (*a*), they are found mostly at the beginning of the poem. As in Valerius, Pelias fears an oracle definitely naming Jason (whereas in Apollonius and Pindar an οἰοπέδιλος is mentioned only) so in the Orphic work (55 sqq.).[2] In both poems Jason prays to his guardian goddess, Juno or Hera (see Orph. 61 sqq.).[3] The episode of Chiron and Achilles (394 sqq.)[4] is different from the same in both Apollonius and Valerius, but resembles the latter more than the former. The Ἀκτορίδης of Orpheus (136)[5] seems due to a misconception of the Actorides of Val. i 407, as Μενοίτιος is named separately. In Orpheus, Aeëtes has an evil dream, goes with Medea to avert its consequences by bathing in the Phasis, and there sees the Argo—all very like Val. v 217 sqq., 330 sqq. Another point worth noting is that the form Erythia, used by Valerius (v 106) for Erythini, appears in Orph. 1051[6] also as the name of a place in the Euxine, though it probably is not there intended to represent Erythini. The mention of Iernis in the latter part of the poem *may*, if my view be correct as regards the scope of the Latin poem, be due to some plan of it left behind by Valerius.

---

[1] Walter Coventry Summers, *A Study of the Argonautica of Valerius Flaccus* (Cambridge: Deighton, Bell, & Co., 1894). The following notes are mine.—J.C.

[2] See p. 3.

[3] See p. 4.

[4] See p. 14.

[5] See p. 7.

[6] See p. 40.

Appendix D
On Ireland and the *Orphic Argonautica*[1]

John D'Alton

The following passage is excerpted from an 1828 essay on Ireland, which won the Cunningham Gold Medal from the Royal Irish Academy, awarded at that time for the best essay published in the Academy's journal. The author assumes a great antiquity for the Orphic Argonautica *and proceeds to speculate on Archaic Greek knowledge of Ireland. Since the OA was actually composed in the fifth century CE (see Appendix B), when Ireland was well-known, such speculation became moot.*

Homer's ambiguous notices shall not be cited at length, though Strabo, Spondanus, and Goropius, consider that a great part of the scenery of the Odyssey is laid in the Atlantic, and Plutarch pronounces an opinion as to the island of Calypso, that may surprise and interest the readers of this Essay, distinctly affirming, that it is "an island five days sail" (in the navigation of these times,) "*to the West of Britain.*"[2] "Nor can any one," says Camden,[3] while he applies the obvious reference to Ireland, "easily conceive why they should call it Ogygia, unless perhaps from *its antiquity,* for the Greeks called nothing Ogygia unless what was *extremely ancient.*"[4] But when Orpheus, the first writer who definitely names Ireland, displaying all the maritime knowledge of his day, in the imaginary route, which he prescribes for Jason and the Argonauts, expressly mentions, *the island of Ireland, its woody surface, its misty atmosphere, &c.* where could he have gleaned his information unless from the Phoenicians.

---

[1] John D'Alton, "Essay on the Ancient History, Religion, Learning, Arts, and Government of Ireland," *Transactions of the Royal Irish Academy* 16 (1830): 27-29. The following explanatory notes are my own.—J.C.

[2] Plutarch, *On the Apparent Face in the Orb of the Moon* 26: "'An isle Ogygian lies far out at sea,' distant five days' sail from Britain, going westwards, and three others equally distant from it..." (trans. C. W. King)

[3] William Camden (1551-1623), English antiquarian and author of *Brittania* (1586), a geography and history of the British Isles.

[4] *Brittania,* "Hibernia" 3. The word "Ogygia" derives from the Greek for "primal" or "primeval."

They, however, who would be Hardouins to Irish Antiquity, suggest two doubts upon this passage, that the Argonautica was not written by Orpheus, and that by whomsoever written, Ireland is not meant by Iernis. As to the first objection, it seems of very little consequence whether the poem was written by Orpheus, Cercops, or Onomacritus, since the very latest of them flourished upwards of five centuries before the Christian era, and to one of these, all agree, the poem must be attributed; and for the second objection, it must here suffice to say, without relying on any internal evidence that might arise from the *great mistiness* ("μεγα νεθος") so consonant with the moisture of the Irish climate,[5] and which, in early days was ascribed rather to magic than to natural causes, that it is repelled by the concurrent interpretation of Camden, the great English antiquarian, the learned Archbishop Usher, the veteran Bochart, Andreas Scottus, Stephanus, and innumerable other antiquaries, and yet more than these, that the course which the poet gives his ship, while it is consistent only with the remotest notions of Geography, and furnishes additional evidence of the antiquity of the poem, brings "Iernis" into view, precisely where Ireland should be discovered; for, on analyzing the poem, the Argo will be traced, after passing through the Bosphorus and Palus Mæotis, as making its way by the Riphaean Mountains, (the Tanais being then thought navigable to the Polar Sea,) into the Northern Ocean; and then returning, rather to diversify the route than with any belief of its reality, by way of the Atlantic to Ireland, from whence the good ship proceeds between the pillars of Hercules into the Mediterranean: the very position of Ireland is denoted with an accuracy, and so named as a landmark of navigation, as would countenance the inference of its being a place then long and well known to mariners.

---

[5] See p. 45, this volume, referring to the cloud surrounding the island of Demeter.

Index

Absyrtus 31, 39-40, 44, 46, 72, 99, 103
Acastus 9, 64, 73
Achilles 15, 17, 77, 86, 112
Actor 8, 63
Admetus 8, 59
Adonis 2
Aegina 7, 77
Aeëtes xii, xiii, xvi, 3, 26, 30-34, 37, 39, 46, 49, 50, 52, 57, 58, 61, 71, 72, 81, 85, 99, 104, 106-108 *passim*; as Oeeta, 85-87 *passim*; as Oeta, 91-93 *passim*
Aeson 3, 4, 5, 11, 19, 22, 23, 31, 36, 45, 51, 57-59 *passim*, 77, 81-82, 86, 88, 92, 93, 94, 103, 107, 108
Aethalides 7, 59
Aether xix, 1
Alcinous 49-51, 72, 107
Amazons 28-29
Amphiaraus 64
Amphidamas 7, 62
Amphion 9, 62
Amphitrite 13
Amycus 26, 68
Anaurus 6, 58, 92
Ancaeus (helmsman) 9, 22, 28, 30, 42, 44-46, 48, 62, 65, 69, 101-104 *passim*, 106
Ancaeus (other uses) 9, 62
Aphrodite 2, 19, 33, 46, 50, 104 (see also Venus)
Apollo 1, 7, 8, 51, 59-61 *passim*, 64, 69, 85, 87, 91, 106; as Paean, 8, 51, 108; as Phoebus 15
Apollodorus xiii, 26
Apollonius of Rhodes x, xi, xiv-xvi, xviii, 7, 26, 29, 36, 49, 53, 60, 61, 63, 65, 99, 110, 112
Aratus 66
Ares xiv, 20, 31-33 *passim*, 41, 87 (see also Mars)
Areius 7
Arete 50, 72, 107
Argo (ship) ix, xii, xvi, xix-xx, 4, 5, 9, 10-11, 14, 19, 21, 27-29 *passim*, 31, 33, 41, 42, 44-45, 48-49, 51, 61, 66, 78, 86, 92, 93, 101, 103, 105-107 *passim*, 112, 140
Argo Navis (constellation) 66, 93
Argonautica (Apollonius) x, xi, xiv-xv, xviii, 29, 36, 49, 53, 60, 63, 65
Argonautica (Valerius Flaccus) xi, xvi, xxi, 112
Argonautica of Orpheus (see *Orphic Argonautica*)
Argonauts (see individual names)
Argus 10-11, 23, 42, 45, 61, 65, 77, 86, 101
Aries 86
Aristophanes xviii, 109
Ark (Noah) xix
Artemis 34-36 *passim*, 41, 100 (see also Diana)
Asclepius 8, 64
Asterion 8, 59, 62
Asterius 9
Athamas 31, 58, 70, 85, 86, 91, 93
Athela 2
Athena xxiii, 2, 4, 11, 19, 21, 22, 27, 33, as Pallas 44, 102 (see also Minerva)
Athenagoras 2
Atlantic Ocean 45, 103, 139, 140
Augeas 9, 62
Ausonian Islands 47, 105, 111

Bacchus 1, 2, 9, 17, 47, 105 (see also Dionysus)
Bacon, Judith xv, xvii, 29, 43
Bebryces 26
Black Sea (Euxine) xv, 5, 28-30 *passim*, 40, 44, 49, 70, 103
Boreas 9, 26, 41

Brimo xix, 2, 17
Bryant, Jacob xx
Bunbury, E. H. 109
Butes 7, 61, 64

Cabiri (see Kabeiroi)
Cadmus 33, 87
Caeneus 8, 60, 64
Calaïs 9, 26, 63, 65, 69
Calliope 1, 5, 27, 53, 59
Camden, William 139
Canthus 7, 60, 65
Casmilus 2
Caspian Sea xv, 40
Castor 7, 22, 36, 62, 79, 92
Catalogue of Women xiii
Catasterismi xvi, 4
Catullus xvi
Cecrops xi, 140
Centauromachy 16
Centaurs 8, 14, 15, 60
Cepheus 9, 62
Ceres 102-104 *passim* (see also Demeter)
Chalciope 30, 33, 57, 58, 65, 70
Chaos xix, 1, 16
Charybdis 48, 110
Chiron 3, 8, 14-17, 112
Cicero 66
Cimmerians 43, 100, 102, 111
Circe xv, 31, 46-47, 52, 104, 108
Cleite 23
Clyteus 60
Colchis xiv, xv, xxiii, 4, 11, 31-33 *passim*, 39, 49, 50, 57, 58, 64, 65, 70, 73, 77-79 *passim*, 81, 85-87 *passim*, 91-94 *passim*, 99
Corcyra xiii, 49, 106
Corinth xiii, 73-74, 81, 83
Corinthiaca xiii
Coronus 7, 60
Creon 74, 83, 87, 95
Crete xvii, 51, 52, 64, 108
Creusa (see Glauce)
Cronian Sea xv, 42, 101, 111

Cronus (Kronos) xviii, xx, 2, 13, 17
Curetes (see Korybantes)
Cyanae 27, 44, 103 (see also Symplegades)
Cybele 2, 21, 70
Cyprus 2, 19, 48, 106
Cyzicus ix, 20, 22-23, 68

D'Alton, John 139
Damascius xix
Dares Phrygius xxi, 76-79
Demeter xi, 2, 13, 43, 45 (see also Ceres)
Deucalion 64
Diana 35, 73
Diké 14
Diodorus Siculus xiv, xvii, 30, 31
Dionysiaca xi, xii
Dionysus (god) xi, xvi-xvii, 2 (see also Bacchus)
Dionysus Schytobrachion (historian) xiv
Dodona, xii, 10, 44
Dragon 33, 71, 81, 84, 86, 87, 92, 93 (see also Serpent)
Dyndimon 21, 23-24

Echion 7, 59
Edmonds, Radcliffe G. vii
Egypt 2-3, 5
Eneus 8
Eos 22
Erginus 7, 62
Eriboetes 60, 65
Erinys 44-45, 52
Eros xix, xx, 1, 16, 34
Erytus 7 (see also Eurytus)
Etna 48, 105, 110
Eumelus xiii
Euphemus 62
Euripides xiv, 74
Eurydamas 8, 60
Eurydice 3, 6
Eurymedon 63
Eurytus 59 (see also Erytus)

Eurytion 60
Euxine Sea (see Black Sea)
Evenus (see Anaurus)

Fabulae (Hyginus) xxi, 7, 56, 57-74
Ficino, Marsilio vii
Fire-Breathing Bulls 33, 71, 81, 87, 93
First Vatican Mythographer xxi, 77, 84-88, 90
Furies 12, 37, 44

Gesner, Johann Matthias vii
Glauce (Creusa) 74, 83, 87, 95
Glaucus 12
Golden Fleece ix, xiv, xv, 4, 30, 31, 34-39, 50, 57, 71, 77, 78, 81, 84-87 *passim*, 90-94 *passim*, 107

Hades (god) 35, 45; as Pluto, 104
Hades (underworld) xvi, 3, 5, 6, 8, 43-44, 102
Hall, Mrs. Angus W. x
Harpes 63, 69
Hecate 35-37
Helios 3, 9, 12, 13, 26, 31, 46 (see also Hyperion and Sol)
Helle 57, 85-86, 91-92
Hellespont 19, 86, 92
Hephaestus 9, 51 (see also Vulcan)
Hera xii, 3, 4, 11, 27, 30-31, 33, 50, 112 (see also Juno)
Heracles xiv, xxiii, 2, 6, 10, 12, 16, 20-21, 22, 24-25, 32, 41 (see also Hercules)
Hercules xi, 61, 63, 64, 66, 79, 87, 92 (see also Heracles)
Hermes 7, 15, 18
Herodotus xi, 41, 111
Hesiod ix, xiii, xix, 1, 37
Hibernia (see Ireland)
Hieroi Logoi (see Rhapsodies)
Hippalcimus 63
Homer ix, xii, xv, 26, 43, 49, 50, 76, 109, 139
Hunter, Richard vii, xiv

Hurst, André xi
Hyginus xxi, 7, 56, 57, 65, 66, 80
Hylas 10, 24-25, 61, 63, 64
Hyperborea 41-42, 100-101, 111
Hyperion 46, 51, 104, 108 (see also Helios and Sol)
Hypsipyle xxi, 18-19, 22, 67

Idaeus 2
Idas 8, 62, 66
Idmon 8, 28, 61, 64, 69
Ierne (Iernis) 44, 45, 111, 112, 140
Iliad xiii, xv, xxi, 26, 50, 76
Ino 57, 85, 91
Iolaus 64
Iolcus (Iolkos) xv, 3, 6, 15, 31, 52, 64, 77, 92, 108
Iphiclus (brother of Thestius) 63
Iphiclus (relative of Meleager) 7, 8, 59
Iphidamas (see Amphidamas)
Iphitus (son of Naubolus) 7, 63
Iphitus (son of Eurytus) 60
Ireland ix, xvii, 44, 103, 111, 139-140 (see also Ierne)
Island of Demeter (Ceres) 45, 103, 111, 140

Jason ix, xii, xiv-xvi *passim*, xix, xxiii, 3-53, 57-74, 76-79, 81-82, 84, 86-88, 90, 92-95, 103-108, 112, 139
Juno 58-59, 70-71, 81, 85, 91, 107, 112 (see also Hera)
Jupiter xxiii, 62, 69, 86, 99, 104, 106 (see also Zeus)

Kabeiroi xxiii, 2, 18
Korybantes 2, 70
Kingsley, Charles x
Kykeon 13

Lactantius Placidus xxi, 80-83
Laocöon 62
Laodocus 7
Laomedon xiv, 78-79, 87

Lake Maeotis xv, 40, 100, 110, 140
Lapiths 8, 15
Lemnos ix, 2, 18-19, 22, 67
Libethra 3, 53, 108
Libya 5, 7, 65
Liber 57, 61, 63, 82, 85, 88, 94
Lucan 93
Lycus 28, 64, 67, 68-69
Lynceus 8, 45, 62, 65, 103

Macrobii (Macrobians) 42-43, 101, 111
Maeotis (see Lake Maeotis)
Maleia 47, 52, 105
Mars 57, 58, 63, 71, 86, 87, 92, 100 (see also Ares)
Medea ix, xiii, xiv, xv, xxi, xxiii, 30-31, 33-53, 58, 60, 65, 70-74, 81-83, 87-88, 93-95, 99, 103-108
Medea (play) xiv, 74
Meleager 7-8, 63
Menoetius 8, 60
Metamorphoses xxi, 80
Migotto, Luciano vii
Minerva xxiii, 66, 72, 81 (see also Athena)
Minyans (Minyae) 5-53 *passim*, 64, 100-108 *passim*
Mopsus 7, 35, 37, 60, 65
Musaeus xi, xvii, 1, 3, 12, 28, 33, 45, 51, 103, 108
Mycenaeans xiii, 6

Narrationes 80
Naupactia xiii, 30
Nauplius 9, 61
Neleus 64
Nelis, Damien P. xviii
Nemesis 99
Nephele 85, 91
Neptune 57, 58, 60-62 *passim*, 64, 66, 69, 81, 92, 106, 108 (see also Poseidon)
Nereus 13, 48
Nilsson, Martin xii

Nonnus xi, xii
Nösselt, Friedrich x
Nostoi xiii
Nurses of Liber 82, 88, 94

Ocean (river) 14, 21, 41, 42, 44, 45
Ocean(us) (god) xviii, 13, 20
Odyssey xii, xiii, 49, 139
Oeagrus 5, 53, 66, 108
Oeeta (Oeta) (see Aeëtes)
Oileus 8, 60
Olympus xviii, 18, 53, 59
Ogygia 139
Onomacritus xi, 99, 109, 140
Orpheus (mythological figure) ix, xi, xvi, xvii, xix, 1-53, 59, 64, 66, 78, 99-108, 109, 110, 112, 139, 140
Orpheus of Crotona xi, 109
Orphic Argonautica vii, ix-xii, 1-53, 68, 76, 78, 99-108, 109-111, 112, 139-140
Orphism xvi-xix, 2
Osiris 2
Ovid xxi, 80, 83

Palaemonius 9, 63
Pandora 37
Parca 28, 50, 51
Peleus 7, 14-15, 17, 22, 48, 61, 65-66, 77, 84, 86, 105
Pelias xiv, xvi, 3, 9, 31, 50, 58-59, 64, 73, 77-78, 81-82, 84, 86-87, 92, 107, 112
Pelion 15, 17, 18, 93
Peloponnesus 3, 47, 61-63 *passim*, 77, 86
Periclymenus 7, 62
Persephone xvi, xvii, xix, 2, 6, 43, 45, 103, 110
Petrides, Siegfried x
Phaeacians xvi, 49, 106-107
Phaenomena 66
Phalerus 7, 61
Phanes xix, 1

Phasis 5, 11, 25, 29, 30, 40, 99, 100, 110, 112
Pherecydes xiii
Philoctetes 64
Phineus 26-27, 63, 69-70
Phlias (Phliasus) 8, 61
Phocus 63
Phoenicians 139
Pholoe 16
Pholus 16
Phorcyn 13
Phrixus 26, 31, 33, 57-58, 65, 70, 71, 84-85, 87, 91-92, 93
Pillars of Heracles (Hercules) 47, 105, 111, 140
Pindar xiv, 15, 42, 112
Pirithous 60
Plato xvii
Pliny the Elder 42
Plouton (Pluto) (see Hades)
Plutarch 139
Pollux (see Polydeuces)
Polydeuces (Pollux) 7, 22, 26, 36, 62, 68, 79, 92
Polyphemus 8, 25, 59, 64
Poseidon 8, 9, 13, 31, 48, 52 (see also Neptune)
Praxidike 2
Preston, William vii, x, 99
Priasus 63
Proteus 13

Ram (Golden) 57, 77, 85, 86, 91-92
Rhapsodies xvii, xviii
Rhea xviii, 21, 23-24

Samothrace 2, 18
Sea of Azov xv, 40
Seaton, R. C. xiv
Second Vatican Mythographer xxi, 90-95
Seneca xiv
Serpent 35-38, 93
Sirens 48-49, 65, 106, 110
Sirius 66

Sol 57, 62-64 *passim*, 71, 81, 91 (see also Helios)
Spartoi 33, 71, 87, 94
Strabo 139
Stymphalides 70
Suda (Suidas) xi, xvii, 109-110
Summers, Walter Coventry 112
Symplegades 27, 69, 70

Taenaron 3, 6, 52, 108
Taking of Oechalia xiii
Talaus 7
Talos 51, 52, 108
Tatian xi, xvii
Taurica xiv, 41, 100, 111
Telamon 8, 61, 66
Theogony (Hesiod) xiii, xix, 1, 37
Thersanon 63
Theseus 60
Thessaly 4, 5, 6, 59, 60, 77, 93
Thetis 15, 48; as Eurybia 105
Thrace 41, 53, 63, 108
Tiphys 6, 11, 14, 17, 19, 20-21, 23, 24, 27, 28, 61, 64, 65, 69, 86, 92
Titans xvii, xix, 2, 20
Triton 13
Trojan History (Dares) xxi, 76-79
Trojan War xiii, xiv, xv, xxi, 19, 76, 78, 79
Troy xiv, 19, 79, 87

Valerius Flaccus, xi, xv-xvi, xxi, 4, 78, 112
Vatican Mythographers (see individual names)
Varro of Atax xv
Venus 65, 67, 71, 107 (see also Aphrodite)
Vian, Francis vii
Vulcan 87 (see also Hephaestus)

West, M. L. xi

Zetes 9, 26, 63, 65, 69

Zeus xvii, xix, xxiii, 2, 6, 8, 10, 11, 17, 20, 21, 26, 35, 37, 40, 45, 48, 49, 86 (see also Jupiter)

About the Translator

Jason Colavito is an author and editor based in Albany, NY. His books include *The Cult of Alien Gods: H. P. Lovecraft and Extraterrestrial Pop Culture* (Prometheus, 2005), *Knowing Fear: Science, Knowledge, and the Development of the Horror Genre* (McFarland, 2008), and more. His research has been featured on the History Channel, and he has consulted on and provided research assistance for programs on the National Geographic Channel (UK), the History Channel, and more. Colavito is internationally recognized by scholars, literary theorists, and scientists for his pioneering work exploring the connections between science, pseudo-science, and speculative fiction. His investigations examine the way human beings create and employ the supernatural to alter and understand our reality and our world.

Visit his website at http://www.JasonColavito.com and follow him on Twitter @JasonColavito.

Printed in Great Britain
by Amazon.co.uk, Ltd.,
Marston Gate.